# INKLINGS

## IRENE BUCKLER

TRUTH SERUM PRESS

First published as a collection February 2018

Truth Serum Press
32 Meredith Street
Sefton Park SA 5083
Australia

Email: truthserumpress@live.com.au
Website: http://truthserumpress.net
Truth Serum Press catalogue:
http://truthserumpress.net/catalogue/

Cover design by Matt Potter
Author photograph used by permission of the author

ISBN: 978-1-925536-41-6


Also available as an eBook
ISBN: 978-1-925536-42-3

Truth Serum Press is a member of the
**Bequem Publishing collective**
http://www.bequempublishing.com/

I've had the good fortune to devour one of Irene's stories every week for over three years as a flash fiction group member. Irene has the ability to create characters who are funny, lovable, sinister or sad. When her stories begin we're taken on a journey, we're not sure where ... until that final twist. Those twists are the magic of flash fiction writing and Irene creates them with skill and sensitivity.

~ Pat Simmons, author of *52 Twisted Tales*

I've admired Irene Buckler's flash fiction stories ever since first reading her work on the Facebook site, *The 52-Week Flash Fiction Challenge*. Some people may think it's easy to write short/short fiction, but the shorter it is the harder you must strive to make it work. Irene's stories find interesting and satisfying ways to interpret human reactions; exposing vibrant characters' fragilities and strengths in narratives that ring with a sense of shared humanity. Then, in the expected twist endings for this genre, she creates unexpected and splendid *ah-ha* moments to surprise both protagonist and reader. Best of all, Irene's stories do what all good stories hope to do ... pack a punch, then linger in the mind after the reading is done.

~ Sheryl Gwyther, author of *Sweet Adversity* and creator of *The 52-Week Flash Fiction Challenge*

Irene Buckler is a sophisticated writer, with a penchant for history, as well as a sensitive understanding of human relationships. These all seem to seep through each of her stories. Add to this, Irene's intuitive understanding of human relationships, means that you have a work of substance. Some of her stories will take your breath away, others will make you smile, and some are even didactic in nature. All of them, however, reveal the curiosity this author displays about the world around her and the people in it, both current and past, as well as her strong moral compass. I am particularly fond of those stories that deal with the notions of revenge and just rewards, as well as those that were given birth at the juncture of some past literary treasure. I hope that Irene continues to bring us such delightful literary fare.

~ Suzanne Kiraly, Book Whisperer for *www.aussiewriters.com.au*

for Mick and Maria Martin

You know who you are
and what you have done
for all of us.

# CONTENTS

# BEGINNINGS

# SLEEPING DOGS

He bursts headlong into our lives, a slippery squalling infant, and she, who has longed for a child for so long, emerges from childbirth triumphant. A mother, at last, she draws me close and wraps me in the moment with her. This is where our new life as a family can begin.

Beguiled by this tiny human with his downy halo of baby hair and miniature hands that instinctively curl around my forefinger as if he is staking a claim, I sense the possibilities, but I am uncertain. Will he be a cure for what ails us or a sticky plaster covering the festering wound of our disappointments? Childlessness, the source of all the tension between us for so long, will no longer be the issue. The issue now is how we deal with our secrets. I know her secret, but she doesn't know mine. However, she recognises my hesitation.

"I love you so much, Tom," she reassures me, her eyes bright with emotion, "and you will be the best father in the world. I know it. "

This is not the time to tell her that I am sterile nor to discuss infidelity, but she is right. I will be a good father.

We name our son Thomas.

# MISSION ACCOMPLISHED

He is a methodical man, who leaves nothing to chance. Accordingly, he has rehearsed each step and is well prepared for the task ahead. He's already checked and double-checked to ensure that everything he might need is within easy reach and all the prerequisites laid out in the appropriate order.

However, what he did not anticipate is the pressure cooker environment in which he is expected to work, the high-pitched urgency that has built to an ear-splitting crescendo as he approaches.

With his confidence levels plummeting, his words come back to haunt him.

"When you come home, you can put your feet up and leave everything to me," he'd promised because it had all seemed so simple at the time.

Gingerly, he leans to begin, but his gorge quickly rises, and he gags.

"I think we have a situation here," he calls out, but she is fast asleep.

Given no choice except to finish what he started, the loving partner and doting new father changes his baby son's soiled nappy.

# IMMORTAL

As a boy, he would pore over his collection of rocks and stones, arranging his specimens by type, in neat rows. He loved the cool quietness of them, their earthy smell and the feel of their weight in the palm of his hands. Barring some cataclysm, rocks and stone last forever and that's what he liked best of all. Now a monumental stonemason, he's much more than a craftsman: he's an artist. In his steady-as-a-rock hands, chisels become precision instruments etching the most ornate letters and decorative shapes into the unyielding surface of stone. For this job, though, his fingers tremble as he uncovers the exquisite white marble block.

This project is more important to him than any he has ever done before. Instead of working with a slab, he'll be working with a block. He won't be creating the letters and words of an elegant epitaph with borders or scrolls, either. This time, he'll be sculpting a memorial. Taking a moment to reflect, he rests his flushed cheek on the calm chill of the marble. Then he begins, scoring the surface to delineate the unwanted marble that he will cut away. He's already beginning to see her. She's locked inside the marble and over the months ahead, he will dedicate himself to coaxing her out into the light. He's been so lonely since she died, but he's bringing her back and this time she'll be immortal.

# FEEDING THE BIRDS

When fat raindrops splatter onto the path in front of her, making wet polka-dots on the warm asphalt, she puts down her heavy shopping bag, opens her umbrella and sucks in the earthy, particle-rich vapour rising into the air. She loves the fresh smell of rain, but she's glad the shower passes quickly, too.

Parting the bracken, she leaves the path. Though she's been here numerous times over the past fortnight and knows exactly where she is going, she treads carefully. On this slope, the terrain is overgrown, and the ground is slippery, particularly after rain, but she's in no hurry. Nowadays, her time's her own and although she's on a mission, she stops every now and again to enjoy glimpses of the tiny bush birds – spotted pardalotes, weebills and fire-tailed finches – that inhabit this secluded place.

Her presence at the bottom of the gully interrupts a chorus of striped marsh frogs in the creek, but she stays just long enough to empty her shopping bag into a natural hollow in the ground. Her husband's frozen head fits into it perfectly. While she expects the crows and magpies will peck at it soon enough, she doubts if anyone will find it, or his other bits and pieces, until she's long gone.

At her age, it's an arduous climb back up to the path, but this was the last of him and she's already feeling ten years younger.

# BUTTERFLY

If my side of our wardrobe is a jam-packed riot of textures and colours, Tom's is a quiet oasis of coordinated neutrals. This is partly because, like all other men, Tom inhabits a far less capricious space in fashion than I do and, consequently, he has far fewer garments to accommodate. However, it's also because he doesn't need any more clothes to impress me. Tom always looks just right dressed in the ones he already owns.

When Tom wears his tuxedo, he's as suave as James Bond. In tweed, he's as smoking hot as Idris Elba and in a perfectly tailored suit, he's as hip as David Beckham.

Leaning into the soft leather bomber jacket that he recently purchased, I take a moment to enjoy the lingering aura of Tom's understated cologne before I decide what to do.

A bomber jacket … what middle-aged man goes out in a bomber jacket?

Now I know that Tom has a lover. In leather, he's turned out to be as selfish as any other two-timing Lothario. His clothes bundled, bagged and donated to a local charity, I am reclaiming his side of the wardrobe for myself.

In my brand new, psychedelic-print kaftan, I am ready to spread my wings and fly solo.

# SAM

Though we had been together for little more than a decade, I could not see myself ever recovering from losing Tony. Over the course of my lifetime, I have been disappointed many times, but never with Tony. I could trust him completely. When I was in one of my moods, Tony didn't judge me. If my hair was oily or bedraggled or my face full of pimples, Tony didn't shy away from me. Tony didn't seem to notice when I put on weight or when I was wearing daggy clothes. Whatever happened, Tony loved me – even when I loathed myself. When he died, our home fell silent and life is not the same without him.

There will never be another Tony, but I don't want to live the rest of my life alone. It is time to open my heart and try to move on. Even so, I hesitate as I reach into the cane basket that my son and daughter have carried between them into the room.

"I can't get used to not having Tony around," my son tells me as my fingers find the furry bundle they have brought. "This house isn't a home without a dog."

Am I about to fall in love with a puppy? I see that he is not just any puppy – and he's not Tony, but we are instantly simpatico. Welcome home, Sam.

# FERTILE GROUND

He remembers when he first stumbled across the old stone wall in a deserted part of the woods. He desperately wanted to know what was on the other side, but was frightened off by the wall's grim guard of grotesque trees with knots and whorls that twisted into scary goblin eyes and mouths.

Years later, the wall is overgrown and still protected by an imposing phalanx of trees, but he is no longer a superstitious child. Carefully parting the bracken to avoid thorny branches that reach out to scratch at his exposed skin, he uses footholds in the old stonework to inch his way to the top of the wall, and drops down on the other side. There he finds an exquisite topiary garden. A leafy green chicken, a dog, a cat, a horse, a cow, a mouse, a swan, a goose and a goat: an impressive display that is tended by an ancient woman, wielding a pair of secateurs. Although he's trespassing, she greets him with a gummy smile.

"I am the gardener," she says, extending her free arm to shake his hand.

Never expecting to find anything beyond the wall other than a continuation of the woods, he's taken aback by the wonders that surround him. He's seen topiary before, he tells the gardener, but never encountered artistry like hers. Each topiary sculpture is anatomically perfect.

"I have my secret ways," the gardener confesses, her eyes inscrutable under the shade of her battered, straw hat, "Each of my plants is unique."

The topiary dog, she explains, was once her favourite working dog, the topiary cat, her greatest mouser and the topiary chicken, the best layer she ever had.

"So, you've based your work on actual animals," he concludes.

The gardener nods, leaning in as if to share a confidence with him.

"Exactly," she whispers.

Plunging her secateurs deep into his neck, the gardener severs his carotid artery with one snip. She's been waiting so long for a human to drop in and add to her collection. Now she can't wait to plant him – with a yew tree, she thinks – and shape him as he grows.

# MONKEY SEE

I'm always drawn to the same family portrait, a happy snap taken years ago in the garden of the old house. When I close my eyes, I can still feel the warmth of the spring sunshine on my arms and smell the jasmine, dripping off the trellis in the background. Standing on either side of my parents like cheeky monkey bookends, my sister and I are beguiling the camera with our gap-toothed smiles and goofy poses.

Though we are forever captured, my sister and I, in our carefree silliness, today the lens of hindsight focuses my attention on my parents. My father has his arm around my mother's waist, but when I look closely, I can see that he is not so much embracing her, as he is pinning her to his side. My father was a controlling husband. Stern and narrow-minded, he stifled my mother. She has since admitted to me that she no longer loved him when the photograph was taken and, yet, she stayed.

When pressed, my mother explains that her love for her daughters was much greater than her resentment of our father and that is why she persevered, but that's not my way. Having unwittingly graduated from a controlling father to a controlling husband of my own, our bags are packed. My cheeky monkeys and I deserve better.

# SMILE

He can hardly wait to uncover her each morning. Her dainty toes are first to emerge. Then his eyes meander along the tops of her feet to her ankles, before following the curve of her calves and up her thighs to arrive at the swell of her hips. Momentarily, he allows his fingertips to touch hers where her hands rest modestly over her pubic mound, before gently raising the covers over her breasts and draping them over her shoulders. Taking a step back from the table, he considers her fine proportions and classic posture. He is well pleased, but the best is yet to come for when he finally lifts the veil to reveal her face, she is smiling. Indeed, all the ladies in this private gallery are smiling at him, just the way he likes it.

"Good morning to you, my little lovelies," he says, bowing ever so slightly.

Unperturbed by the cruel deformities that see him shunned by society, his ladies smile and watch in silent admiration as he moistens his hands and sculpts her hair, moulding the porcelain clay into delicate waves that spill onto her shoulders and beyond. She is his finest creation. He will call her Venus and she will take pride of place when she joins the others.

A grand master, his pottery pieces are highly sought after by collectors of fine art. However, his ladies are not for sale.

# THE ARRANGEMENT

Bristling with indignation, I back away from the tangle of well-wishers fawning over Sameek, the Guptas' relative, newly arrived from India. I'm only here because I couldn't resist the onslaught of my parents' desperate entreaties, but I don't have to like it.

"No pressure," they promised me in honeyed tones. "Absolutely no pressure at all."

Who are they kidding? Everyone knows I'm here for one reason only and I'm so embarrassed. My parents and the Guptas are convinced that this stranger, this Sameek, and I are a match made in heaven. According to my parents, he's a real catch! I don't bother asking how they could know that, but studying Sameek from a safe distance, I note his short stature, large hawkish nose and fat-lobed ears. A preening rooster strutting around the henhouse, his snorts of laughter bounce around the space between us and I am adamant; I never want to meet him.

Slipping outside into the garden, I encounter another escapee, an earnest young man with a shock of unruly dark hair. Slipping easily into conversation, we discover we are like-minded about match-making.

"I too," he commiserates with me, "Am here to meet someone, but I much prefer your company."

Boldly taking my hand, he reminds me that we are both

adults, free agents and under no obligation to stay. I agree and as we leave, he introduces himself.

"I'm Sameek," he says and, just like that, I realise that, sometimes, my parents can get it so right.

# WORDS

He chooses his words carefully.

"Impractical"

Paired with a disinterested shrug, he uses the word to dismiss me and that's it. The subject is closed, and he looks away to resume watching a televised game. There's always another game to watch and the practicalities of the choices he makes are never questioned.

"Unnecessary"

Strictly speaking, he's right. We have all that we need, but he generally gets what he wants, as well, and anyway, it wouldn't hurt him to hear me out before turning back to whatever he's doing on the computer.

"Selfish"

With this he raises one eyebrow, giving me that crooked half-smile of his, the one that says he knows I'm not being serious; that we're sharing an inside joke. I'm not joking, but if there's a way to accuse someone of being selfish without sounding harsh, my husband knows it. Chastened, I wonder for the umpteenth time, if I have my priorities right.

Though softly spoken, his words are corrosive. The acid rain of his tacit disapproval targets my aspirations. He's a clever man, but this time he underestimates my resolve. My inner voice is too persuasive.

"Challenge, opportunity and independence!" it says.

Today, I am wife and mother, and tomorrow — who knows what words I will use to describe myself? I am resuming my studies, whether he likes it or not.

# A MATTER OF FACT

"No man can fathom God's plan!" Father John booms from the pulpit, his chins spilling over his tight clerical collar as he speaks.

One look at us, my threadbare mother and her pinch-faced brood of ragged children, is enough for me to fathom God's plan for girls like me and to reject it. I stifle a yawn and my mother pins my squirming siblings to their seats with her fiercest glares, compelling them to attend. Faith is very important to women like my mother, who have little else to sustain them. She wants us to absorb every word that Father John utters.

"For my yoke is easy and my burden light," he drones, steepling his fat fingers. "Let us pray."

Her chapped hands clasped together over her distended belly, my mother bows her head, but I know – and Father John knows, too – that no amount of devotion or prayer will enable her to put more food on our poor table, buy new shoes, warm coats and medicine for her sickly children or convince the church to lift its embargo on birth control. This baby will be her tenth. Her yoke will never be easy, nor her burden light, but things will be different for me.

I put my faith in science and have accepted the first fulltime scholarship ever awarded to a girl in our parish. I have my own plan.

# WINNER TAKES ALL

We could not be more different, he and I, yet we cannot resist each other. Though my family and friends disapprove, we marry and leave our critics behind, cocooning ourselves in cosy coupledom, but exclusivity changes us. As I withdraw from the naysayers, I become dependent on him and while I am wrapped in the warm blanket of young motherhood, he quietly assumes control. Only when I decide I am ready to return to work, do I realise the mistake I have made.

Though I am chafing against the narrow confines of my life, he won't allow me to work. He doesn't want our young son and daughter in childcare.

"Your job is wife and mother," he insists.

The issue festers, but we set aside our differences to visit his parents overseas. They gush over their son and our children, but when they meet me, the disappointment shows in their eyes. I am a foreigner and not what they want for their son. However, their veiled criticism only hardens my resolve and on our return home, I find a job and book the children into childcare.

Relieved when he volunteers to drop them on his way to the office, I blow them a kiss as they drive away. He waves goodbye and they are gone.

I think I've won the battle, but while I put in my first day at work, they are leaving the country. The war has only just begun.

# THE STOPOVER

I can only marvel at the journey that has brought me here to this privileged world, where my every whim is indulged, where nothing is too expensive, where the chauffeur is always on call and the private jet is always on standby. My fiancé's vast rural estate with its lush formal gardens is a glittering emerald in a thirsty landscape. I never imagined that life could ever be like this. Who could ask for more?

When I tripped and fell at a crowded railway interchange, it was Jim who helped me to my feet. What were the chances, I wonder, of our paths intersecting at that very moment in time, of Jim and me walking away together and of me ending up here? Yet this is where I am, two years later, preparing to marry the fabulously rich and charming Jim, who loves me dearly.

The sky is churning black as I slip into my shimmering white gown and a sob is building in my throat because I'm no longer in love with Jim.

From my window I see a car in the distance, a promise kept. There is only one thing to do.

I kick off my shoes, gather my skirts and run barefoot across the manicured lawns to the parched fields beyond, where a disused freight line marks the way out of town.

The handsome chauffeur is waiting.

# STARTING OVER

On this stifling January night, even her pillow is hot, but that is not why she cannot sleep. Her brain is on fire. She hates starting at a new school, being the newbie – finding new friends, establishing herself and learning new rules and routines. More than that, though, she worries about making the right impression and being able to handle the type of bullies that had made her previous school such a misery.

She tries to distract herself by concentrating on the mundane, the details she can control. Her clothes are ready, and she has packed everything she could possibly need: a variety of books and loads of stationery, a morning snack and her lunch. That done, she is back to worrying, agonising over the challenges she will face and rehearsing responses to them – and so it goes until, at last, she slips into a sweaty slumber.

Within hours she is calming herself as she opens her new classroom door. Armed with the wisdom of hard lessons learnt, she is determined to prevail.

"Good morning, boys and girls," she announces, her voice rising above the steady hum of overhead fans. "I am your new teacher."

# COFFEE BREAK

As she approaches, you think you might see the ghost of her smile resurrected on her lips, but it's gone before you can be sure. Then, not wishing to pre-empt her, you look down, pretending to be preoccupied with your phone.

"Coffee?" you ask.

Although neither of you wants a cup, you've always enjoyed the coffee at this café and, after all, you can't occupy a table without buying something.

Glancing back at her as you wait at the counter to be served, you are filled with admiration. Nobody here would suspect the resilience that underpins her composure or the tortured path she has travelled to reach this point.

"Okay?" you enquire.

She is taking a sip of her skinny latte, but you're not interested in the coffee. She knows that. Had you been different people, you would have accompanied her. She knows that, too, but she's never let her illness define her. Needing a support person is not part of her narrative.

The wait has been excruciating, but this time, there is no mistake. She looks at you and declares her victory over her cancer in a sunburst, a smile that floods your world with light. There are no words, nor any need for them.

# THE CLEANSING

I return to the river to flush away the misery that plagues me and to find hope again, but her magic is no longer working, as it once did for me when I was a child. As the tips of my toes touch the water, I am drawn by the way the ripples distort my reflection. Even the river mocks me with the twisted being I have become. More than ugly, I am grotesque.

Somewhere in the distance, a magpie calls. Its song, a plaintive solo, hangs above the rustling chorus of foliage along the riverbank as I slip into the shallows and head for deeper water, my intolerable burden of despair resting heavily on my shoulders. When I can no longer touch the riverbed, I throw back my arms and surrender.

I give up. I cannot go on.

I am weightless and floating in Mother Earth's amniotic waters. Somewhere in the deepest recesses of my mind, my brain suggests that my natural buoyancy has saved me, but my heart knows otherwise. As I make for the riverbank, I offer up my locket to the river in tribute, and as the golden chain slides through my fingers into the deep, I see the light again and I can smile.

# COMPLICATIONS

# SOLSTICE

On Midsummer's Eve we sit around our campfire, two couples in awe of the endless Outback night and its infinite bounty of twinkling stars. Kakadu is a spiritual place.

I shudder, my superstitious core touched by an unexpected frisson of Dreamtime magic.

"Let's build a bonfire like our ancestors did – to protect us from bad spirits," I suggest, and everyone thinks it would be great fun.

The surrounding scrub is dry and makes excellent fuel. As soon as our bonfire is ablaze, we break out the whiskey and settle in to toast the summer solstice, but soon our carousing gives voice to old jealousies and secrets best forgotten. The night ends bitterly.

We are subdued in the morning. In bruised silence, we break camp and pack our cars. We drive away in opposite directions, over the ashes of our friendships, the scrub we destroyed and a scattering of empty bottles.

No bonfire can protect us from the bad spirits of our own making.

# NO CHARGE

When the box arrives, we are so excited that we drag it inside and empty it immediately. We remove metres of bubble wrapping and spread the doll-like component parts across the floor, eager to begin.

Our Stepford Sanitation Sally's legs, complete with fully articulated ankles and knees, slip seamlessly into her torso. However, as we attach her jointed arms, with their celebrated five-fingered-softest-hands-with-opposable-thumbs feature for the personal grip for which her model is so renowned, our Sally topples forward. We struggle to hold her upright as we slot her sensor box into the place where her head will go as soon as we can afford to upgrade to the full facial model.

In her lightweight uniform and with her fifth-generation multi-mop in its purpose-built pocket along her back, she would be ready to plug in, charge up and start cleaning, if only Stepford had sent a compatible, ultra-dynamic, predictive A/C charger with our order.

We can't wait to see our Sally strut her stuff and hope the Stepford Customer Service Department can rectify the matter swiftly.

# SURVIVOR

My village is rooted in the side of a mountain, far from the nearest town. Visitors are rare, and the arrival of the traveller causes great excitement. We are always hungry for news — hopefully of Papa, who is away — and we crave the novelty of fresh company, but this traveller brings something more.

We gather to welcome him, but the traveller sickens as we prepare a feast in his honour. His death is swift. We burn his body, but it is already too late to stop the contagion spreading. Our priest tells us to pray for forgiveness from our Heavenly Father because the contagion is His punishment for our sins. We beg for our lives, even as we drop, and now everyone is gone, except for me.

If there is any comfort in being the sole recipient of divine forgiveness, it is that now no one can stop me climbing the great tree. No one is alive to worry if I dangle by my hands from the branch that overhangs the village churchyard or to warn me that if I let go, it will be a mortal sin and unforgiveable. I am suspended in a place between Heaven and earth — unclaimed by either. However, as I inch further outwards, the supple branch bows and the great tree deposits me safely onto the soft ground below.

Come home soon, Papa. Please.

# CHEERS

My local, a warm oasis on this wintry night, draws me in from the cold. Inside my friends' familiar laughs rise above the Friday night hubbub of mirth and merriment; we girls are a tight knit group. Delayed at work, I am one of the last to arrive and as I walk in, shrugging off my heavy coat, I see that the others have not wasted any time. The table around which they are gathered is already piled up with bottles, glasses and half-eaten snacks.

I make a quick detour to the bar to get a drink. The girls are even noisier now and I am dying to know who they are talking about. Then, as I make my way through the crowd, I make eye contact with one and she beckons me over, which should feel wonderful except that her friendly gesture also seems to act as a warning to the others. Their laughter abruptly stops. Everyone looks at me, and for a moment, I am on the outer, but just as suddenly, they relax and are all sparkly-giggly again.

"Oh, it's you Sally," gushes Corinne, one of my best friends. "We thought for a moment that you were Joanne."

That's a relief. In from the cold in more ways than one, I can now happily cosy up with the others as we toast absent friends – and talk about them.

# ON TOP OF THE WORLD

The view from the summit is breathtaking. The city, far below is a Lilliputian jewel against a majestic coastline that meanders into the distance.

"Worth the climb?" he asks as they drink it all in.

Out of puff from the last and steepest part of their ascent, she simply nods as they stand together on the lofty rocky outcrop, defying the biting wind that nips at their faces and fingers. His arms encircling her protectively from behind, she leans back into the secure warmth of his embrace.

As their wedding anniversary approached, she had been both surprised and delighted when he had suggested the climb – just the two of them, a chance to get away from everyone else and reconnect. Although not a climber, she recognised that having time alone, was just what they needed to revitalise their struggling marriage and now, at this very moment, on top of the world, they are as one again.

"I love you," she murmurs.

His arms clamp tightly around her as he lifts her off her feet and nobody hears her scream as she plummets to her death.

He is comforted by all their friends and family after the tragic loss of his wealthy young wife. They think they understand when, heartbroken, he announces his intention to relocate to Hawaii.

# SWALK

He's been gone far too long, and she misses him more and more with each passing day. His socks are still stuffed in his drawer. His jackets still hang in the closet and his old slippers still languish under his side of their bed, but his things only serve to remind her that he is not there. Even their framed wedding photos upset her – he and she are like specimens, held under glass to study. She can look. She can remember, but she cannot touch him – and she wants, so much, to touch and be touched. Her skin is hungry. She is starving for him.

Now the thought of seeing him again consumes her. She flushes with excitement as she takes her favourite lipstick, 'Carmine', the very deepest of reds, and applies it generously, first to her plump bottom lip and then to the other. Mirror in hand, she scrutinises her reflection, pouting and posing, until she is satisfied that her lips are perfect.

He will soon be home. She is sure of it, but in the meantime, she plants a creamy kiss on the envelope and sends him her love in a letter – as she does every day.

Note: The acronym S.W.A.L.K. (sealed with a loving kiss) was commonly used in letters to and from those serving on the front line in World War II.

# DREAM GIRL

"Ouch!" Chad exclaims. "Paper cut."

He drops the offending paperwork and thumps his desk in anger.

"Just as well it's nothing serious," observes his bemused colleague, an older man called Ben, sitting opposite.

Chad knows his reaction is over-the-top, but the paper cut is not the real problem. Their new receptionist is the real problem. From his office he sees her sitting with one long leg crossed over the other, accentuating the curve of her calf, which draws his gaze down to her ankle and her impossibly high stiletto-heeled shoes. The real problem is that instead of paying attention to what he was doing, he had been watching her – as he always does. She is the reason for the paper cut, the proposals piling up, the desk thumping and the time wasted fantasising over her.

"It's all about her," Chad admits, nodding towards their receptionist. "I knew she was trouble the moment she walked into the office looking like that."

To make matters worse for Chad, their receptionist has done nothing at all to encourage him, except of course, to look and move the way she does. If anything, it appears to Chad that she might have gone out of her way to avoid him. Since Ben hired her and introduced them nearly a week ago, they have hardly spoken to each other. She has been conscientiously applying herself to her new job, while he has been distracted from his.

Ben is not immune to the receptionist's charms, either. Although she is a very articulate and efficient young woman, who came highly recommended, he knows that her physicality swayed him to offer her the position.

"She's a very pretty girl, but let's face it, you have no idea who she really is and what she is really like," he cautions, but Chad is not ready to hear Ben's appeal to common sense.

He shakes his head because he knows all he needs to know. His eyes assure him that their receptionist satisfies every criterion demanded by the part of his brain that defines his ideal mate.

Sensing they are talking about her, their receptionist flicks her golden hair over her shoulders and turns her back on Chad and Ben. She retrieves her handbag from the bottom drawer of her desk and stands, rising elegantly, straightening her tiny jacket and smoothing her figure-hugging pencil skirt before approaching Chad's office.

"I'm taking my break now," she informs them, smiling her super model smile.

Ben nudges Chad as she leaves.

"I want you to go after her and strike up a conversation," he says firmly and points to the door. "Go!"

The last thing Ben wants in the office is Chad's unresolved sexual tension gumming up the works. Signalling an end to their conversation, he resumes work as Chad heads out the door. He is not surprised when a moment later Chad is back.

"She's out there having a smoke!" Chad announces, recoiling as if he has just been exposed to an infectious disease.

Ben is smiling as Chad puts his head down to catch up on his work. Problem solved.

# MEANT TO BE

I am so haunted by the ghosts of my eternally-unlucky-in-love past that when broad-shouldered Rob, with his beguiling blue eyes and boyish smile, shows an interest in me, a socially awkward and thoroughly beige-coloured singleton, I don't know what it is that he sees in me.

"That's exactly it," he says, dismissing my concerns with a cheeky laugh. "You don't know how special you really are."

With Rob at my side, I am complete, at last. I am his eternally-meant-to-be lover and soul mate, and he is mine. Surrounded by admiring friends and family, we marry. We plan, and we invest. We gain, and we lose, but money is just money. My only real disappointment is that we are childless. Rob convinces me not to worry, to be patient and to give it time. He persuades me that we should have fun in the meantime, while we can — and so we do.

I thought our love would last forever, but one day, Rob disappears. The police investigation establishes that Rob — not his real name — is a conman, known to them as a serial bigamist. So, I am not legally married, and I never was. I no longer wonder what an irresistibly charismatic, but penniless man sees in an unremarkable, but desperate woman, whose best feature is her money. I just wonder what I am to do now that I am penniless, too.

# THE REAL DEAL

With its intricate pattern of flowers and curlicues, the ring is truly lovely. If there's one thing about George, it's that he understands what I like – and I adore damascene etching.

"This was my grandmother's," he tells me, softly placing the precious ring on my open palm, "And I want you to have it."

Now that his affair is over, George wants me to take him back and he searches my face for signs of encouragement. He does not have to tell me how much he needs me. We both know that without me behind him, he will be unable to finance his business ventures.

The gold ring sits heavily in my hand, a potential bridge between our past and the future George hopes to share with me. George says he loves me and I am sure he's confident that the gift of a family heirloom will be the deal maker.

"One day, we will have a daughter for you to pass it on to," he continues, deftly tapping into my hopes and dreams. "Come on. What do you say?"

What I don't say is that I know George bought the antique ring on eBay or that I had it on my watch list and would have bought it for myself if he hadn't beaten me to it. I am relocating to another city with another man, but I don't tell George that either. I just leave with my new ring and say I will think it over.

# PLANS

I'm not looking for love, but when our eyes meet we connect so powerfully that I find it hard to look away. For someone who has lost the inclination to seek new relationships, the sudden stirring of long sublimated emotions is disorienting and almost enough to make me linger, but not quite. I have plans for the day.

Mindful that I should be working on several important briefs, I hurry away, trying to concentrate on the plus side of the equation of my life: the kudos that comes from being a celebrated barrister, the bulging property and investment portfolio and having more money than I know how to spend, but it's not working. The down side of my life is that I've been going home to an empty house for far too long and although I like to think I am completely self-sufficient, I suddenly find myself haunted by a possibility. I really want him.

Like a silly schoolgirl, I rush back. He's still there and minutes later he's in my arms. He's mine – my puppy, my Harry. Plans change.

# PLAY TIME

She glances up from her laptop to discover that while she's been on Facebook, her five-year-old son, Tom, has obviously been poking around where he's not allowed to be. He should be in trouble, but he looks too adorable.

"What's that on your head?" she asks.

The stainless-steel pasta strainer has never looked so cute.

"My helmet," he says, but his look says she's asked a silly question, "I'm a space ranger."

Tom zooms away on his planet hopper. His father's most expensive golf club has never seen such cosmic action and she would see the funny side if it wasn't for the fact that the golf club has come from the garage and the garage is strictly out-of-bounds for Tom. She calls him over.

"But I'm chasing a brain sucker," Tom insists, stopping momentarily to brandish his alien blaster as his mother's eyes widen in horror.

Tom has his father's pistol. The garage is full of dangerous things.

"Die, brain sucker!" he says, taking aim.

The gun discharges. Tom is knocked off his feet and she drops to the floor as the bullet finds its mark. Her laptop is obliterated.

"It's okay, Mummy," he reassures her as they pick themselves up. His bright little face is beaming. "The brain sucker's dead. Now you can play with me."

# GAP YEAR

My sister and I wander around Westminster Abbey, the Houses of Parliament and Big Ben, our hushed conversations steamy in the frosty December air.

We buy a tin of caramel toffees in Harrods to sweeten the prospect of joining the crowd of shoppers milling around the Christmas window displays outside. Just after 4pm, when it is dark, we gape in wonder, swaddled in our warm coats, scarves and beanies, at the dazzling web of twinkling Christmas lights that stretches overhead from one end of Regent Street to the other.

The forecast is for snow and as we make our way back to the tube station, a snowflake landing on my cheek delivers winter's sweetest kiss. For two young Aussies backpacking around Europe, this last stop in London is a dream coming true. We can decorate with real holly, build a snowman, put out crumbs for robin redbreasts and enjoy a traditional Christmas dinner in mid-winter – or we could if either of us was able to cook such a meal.

Beneath her bright smile, I see a familiar faraway look in my sister's eyes when I suggest we book for Christmas dinner at a restaurant with an open fire.

"Not going to be the same without Mum's cooking, though," she says and I cannot disagree.

Despite the allure of a white Christmas, we both know it's time for us to go home.

# COLLECTOR

For a blind date, she must admit this one's been a corker. The physical attraction between them had been immediate, their over dinner conversation so satisfying that she had easily been persuaded to come back here, to his place.

Anticipating the hours ahead, she sinks into the sofa and sighs with pleasure. Everything feels just right. While he's in the kitchen making the coffee, her eye is drawn to an ornately enamelled keepsake box on an elegant side table. She wonders whether it would be rude to look inside, but not for long enough to stop her opening it up to see.

Inside is a single tooth, not a stubby baby tooth, but an adult one with a long root. She is both repulsed and puzzled, even more so when she notices other boxes in the same style displayed around the room.

Her last living thought is that she won't ever trust first impressions again.

He tilts back her lifeless head, so that her mouth falls open and he can see each of her perfect teeth.

Now which one will he take as a keepsake?

# WELCOME HOME

Against a backdrop of steely grey, the old man is a lonely figure, windblown and tiny against the vast stretch of sand. He is waiting – hoping – dreaming of a golden past, sunshiny days spent here with her. She is still the love of his life. He remembers the pledges and promises they made. He would return from war he told her. Like the waves that must roll endlessly to shore, he would come back – and it is so, but many years have passed.

At last, she has his letter and, finally, she knows his awful secret. She knows what he lost in battle. She knows they could never have enjoyed a full life or had children together. She knows why he set her free.

The old man clutches her short, unsigned reply as he follows the progress of a woman wandering along the water's edge, leaving a long and meandering trail of footprints in her wake. She approaches and with each closing step, she becomes more familiar, impossibly so – she is much too young.

When she reaches him, the woman stops.

"This is a special place for me," she says.

The old man dares to hope.

"My mother asked that her ashes be scattered on this sand," the woman continues.

His thin shoulders sag. He is too late, but she takes his hand

and her warmth flows through him.

"I answered the letter you wrote to her," she says, softly, "You're my father. Welcome home, Dad."

# SECRETS

I lead the way and after an exhilarating climb, we are high on the escarpment in a sheltered niche overlooking the plains far below. Although we haven't known each other long, I knew as soon as I saw Zoe that I wanted to bring her to my secret place. She hesitates when I push aside the woody shrubs to reveal a narrow gap between the boulders, but with a little reassurance she is close on my heels as I squeeze through the gap into the claustrophobic space and crawl towards to the cave beyond.

Once inside, I'm able to stretch to my full height and I'm ready to help Zoe to her feet as she joins me.

"I'm the only person in the world who knows about this place," I say, drawing her close.

Her breath is warm on my cheek.

"Not anymore," she whispers, but she is mistaken.

As her eyes adjust to the darkness, I feel Zoe's muscles tense as she focuses in on my display, a perfectly matched set of the most magnificent blond ponytails ever to have graced a human head – except for hers. Her recoil is electric, but even as she clutches at her remarkable hair, my hands have her throat in a vice-like grip and I am exploding with the thrill of the kill.

Foolish girl – my secrets are not for sharing.

# SHOW STOPPER

From their front row seats in the small theatre, Papa and Sophie can see everything. Fascinated by the artistry that underpins the performance, Papa analyses the magician's every move, while Sophie swoons at his handsome looks.

Rabbits and doves appear out of impossible places only to vanish into others. Objects defy the laws of gravity, levitating on the magician's command, and Papa knows that everything is an illusion, that nothing is real. He is smug when Sophie volunteers to be sawn in half. He is totally relaxed when the magician helps her into a coffin-shaped box from which only her feet and head are visible, but nobody is expecting what comes next.

As soon as he begins to saw, the magician's expression darkens and Sophie starts to scream, stunning the audience into horrified silence. Papa squirms in his seat. When the magician completes the cut, the box separates into two bloody halves.

Papa jumps to his feet.

"Sophie!" he howls, rushing at the stage as the lights go out, plunging the theatre into darkness.

As Papa flails around blindly, the lights go on again, and the audience is on its feet, cheering. Unharmed and smiling, Sophie and the magician are centre stage. Papa joins hands with his daughter and son-in-law and they take a bow.

As always, the finale is a show stopper!

# TIGER

A dog is yapping, making such an awful racket that she throws her hands up in exasperation and stomps outside to confront the culprit.

"Go home, you pest!" she commands, but the dog, a terrier, ignores her.

She is not a people person. They say that she is aloof and friendless, but she is not an animal person, either, and looking at the crazed terrier, she cannot imagine why anyone would want to own such a repugnant creature.

As she is shooing the dog away, she discovers what all the commotion is about. The dog has a kitten bailed up against the courtyard wall, a tiny ball of fury, spitting and hissing, fighting for its life.

"A kitten," she groans, pulling a disdainful face.

Although she loathes cats even more than she dislikes dogs, she has no option but to rescue the kitten from its attacker and her aversion is affirmed in blood when, holding the kitten at arm's length, she is scratched and bitten for her trouble. However, as she searches for a box in which to contain it, the kitten relaxes, and she feels a soft rumbling in its puny chest. Then, as it nestles into the palm of her hand, she finds herself admiring its tigerish markings and her heart melts.

She calls him Tiger and he makes himself at home.

# TALL TALES

# SOUTHERN
# CROSS

Only when the Southern Cross reaches the highest point of its journey across the night sky and the last lights are out in distant farmhouses, do they dare to show themselves. The rarest and most reclusive of all nocturnal creatures, their extraordinary protective colouration and instinctive distrust of humankind have always served them well.

Raising their mossy snouts to test the air for danger and on legs that unfold from beneath their bulbous bellies, they slowly rise from the earth. Moonlight polishing the weathered curves of their backs, they inch their way along to congregate with others of their kind and rub together in companionable silence.

Belly flat to the ground, he is downwind of the herd. With its curious rock formations, this secluded area on the Monaro Plains has always been his favourite getaway. Whenever he is here, he senses the prehistoric magic of the terrain, but he's never been here at night and he's never come even close to suspecting the full wonder of it. Here, the random piles of granite boulders are neither random nor are they granite. Here, they are something entirely different. Here, in the velvet darkness, the very landscape is in motion.

Incredulous, he rubs his eyes to make sure he's not dreaming. He cannot wait to tell the world about the ponderous giants he's discovered, but the hours pass slowly and though he tries to stay alert, he falls asleep, unaware that the herd has caught his scent or that, ever so gradually, it is closing in on him.

With the sun warming him to the core, he sleeps more deeply than ever before. He sleeps through the day and into the following night. Awakening in darkness, he finds himself encircled by the herd and its closeness reassures him in a way that he is slow to comprehend. In its midst, he feels safe and calm. Too exhausted to lift his abnormally heavy head, he dozes again.

Only when the Southern Cross reaches the highest point of its journey across the sky and the last lights are out in distant farmhouses does he find the strength to move. Slowly he rises from the earth on four legs that unfold uncertainly from beneath his bulbous belly and takes his place in the herd.

Searchers may find his abandoned camping gear, one day, along with his clothing and shoes. At one point, they may even scramble over his rocky hide as they poke around looking for clues, but no trace of him will ever be found. Like others – those who came before him – he will keep the secret of this special place, forever.

# THE NECKLACE

Having popped up overnight, the carnival is a tawdry scar on this pristine piece of coastline. At this early hour, though, the little merry-go-round stands still. The popcorn and fairy floss stalls are unmanned, and the battered dodgem car track is silent. Except for a dry husk of a woman, bent with age, who beckons me to her fortune-telling tent, the site is deserted.

Though sceptical, I follow her inside. We sit on opposite sides of a flimsy folding table as she studies my face.

"You think we are alone, my dear, but it is not so," the fragile fortune-teller rasps, her unnervingly opaque eyes locking onto mine as she begins to draw.

Though her movements are automatic, where her pencil glides, sight-unseen across the paper, a face gradually appears and only when the face is fully formed, does the fortune-teller release me from her gaze. Exhausted, she struggles to hand the portrait across the table and orders me to go.

Squinting in the sunlight, I look back over my shoulder. Where the fortune-teller's tent should be, the sand is bare – no merry-go-round, no stalls and no dodgem cars.

Everything has gone, but in my hand, I have my portrait and around my neck the fortuneteller has drawn the distinctive art deco necklace that my great granny always wore in family photos.

Though the beach is now deserted, I am not alone.

# CORNSWOGGLED

Our corn is as high as the sky. Pa says he'll harvest it right soon, but in the meantime to stay out of them fields coz they is dangerous. Course, I ain't worrying about that when I chase after that dog that's chasin' into that corn after the biggest rabbit I ever seen. Only when that dog gets away from me and I stop runnin', do I see I got a problem. All that corn, it be huggin' in real close to me, sharp-like, and I can't figure out which way I should go.

I try to stop thinkin' about that boy that disappeared out here and start tryin' to push my way through the corn, callin' out for m' dog, hopin' he ain't been gobbled up by some monster. Pa says monsters is all bad men and that's all I need to know, but when that corn rustles and sighs, I is ready to believe anythin' and that's why, when my Granny comes outta nowhere and shows me the way home, I ain't askin' her no questions. No siree, and if she been dead since the start of winter, well, I ain't complainin' about that, neither – nor the stink.

Course, that dog's fine, but my Granny and that big rabbit's gone like smoke – and me? Well, I ain't never goin' near them corn fields ever again.

# SISTERS

The stranger in the crowd looks like me and when I take a better look at her, I see that her face doesn't just resemble mine; her face is mine. What is more, we have the same unruly mop of auburn hair, the same strong chin and the same athletic build. My heart thuds. The stranger is my mirror image and that can't be a coincidence. Sure, I've heard that everyone has a double, somewhere, but what are the chances? The distance between us closes and I stop, expectantly, but she is looking at her phone and walks on. I would call after her, but my words stick in my mouth.

Convinced that the stranger must be related to me, I rush home. Is it possible that I have a sister – a twin? Unexpected tears well in my eyes and threaten to trickle onto my cheeks. My home is full of wonderful childhood memories, but now I am desperate to know why she, my maybe-twin, was not part of them. As I fumble in my handbag for my house keys, my mother opens the front door. Her arms outspread to gather me inside with a hug, her demeanour changes when I back away.

"What's wrong?" she asks, but seeing the betrayal in my eyes, I think she already knows.

We've always understood each other, Mum and I, and it's as if she's been preparing for this conversation.

"You've seen her out there," she says, inclining her head towards the street. "Haven't you?"

Taking my hand, she leads me into the kitchen. We always do our best talking there, sitting at the table. She puts the kettle on.

"Is she my twin?" I ask.

If so, I must know the circumstances of our separation and growing up apart. After all, people make difficult choices and I am prepared for any explanation.

"I've seen her, too," Mum admits.

Then, as she pours our tea, she tilts my world on its axis.

"You are not a twin," she says, "You are one of many."

How can I be one of many?

My adoption contract contains an assurance that all other members of my batch would be adopted overseas. So much for that. I am a clone and tomorrow my search for my sisters begins.

# A DROP OF RED

With her head held high and her long, dark hair drawn back into a classic chignon, his wife's bare neck and shoulders gleam like polished alabaster under the lights. He is full of admiration. This evening she is wearing his favourite gown, an elegant creation of the finest crimson silk with a priceless ruby necklace that bleeds into its bodice. Though they have been together for years, his wife is still an exquisite creature. Her beauty is timeless.

"Fancy a drop of red before we go out?" he asks as she joins him.

His question is rhetorical; she will have her usual and, for his wife, only the best will do.

He watches as she raises the flute of chilled AB negative, the very rarest of blood types, to her plump lips and sighs with desire as the tips of her fangs emerge. Preferring his red to be served fresh and at body temperature, he is always anxious to begin their night's work, but spending this quiet time alone before they go out is important to them.

Every marriage is a work in progress, especially one that is centuries old.

# THE UNBORN

But for a silvery shard of moonlight, a luminous line stretching from a chink in the tightly shuttered window to the door, she is in darkness, waiting for the lunacy to pass. The door is all that stands between her and him, her husband. Tonight, he is a dangerous predator. Too frightened to move or to make a sound, she cowers in the corner as the door takes a savage beating. Its reinforced timber groans, but it holds.

"Open up!" he screams, over and over again, with mighty thuds that shake the walls and scraping sounds that tear her heart to shreds.

She blocks her ears. This is not the first time, but she can tell no one. Who would believe that her husband loves her or that he cannot help himself and does not want to hurt her? She knows that if her father could see her husband tonight, he would want to kill him. He would say her husband is a monster.

The waiting is excruciating, but she knows the night will pass and in the morning she will be able to release her husband safely from the cellar. Together they will repair the damage and prepare for the next full moon when he will become the beast, once more. Although she has struggled to come to terms with being married to a werewolf, with their unborn child quickening in her belly, there is no going back.

# TRAPPED

Irresistibly drawn by his smouldering good looks and charm, she finds herself wrapped in the arms of a familiar stranger – one she knows so very well, yet hardly at all. Worse, she is in that place, an exquisite entrapment where reason surrenders to desire. It is not part of the plan, but how could she have anticipated that her every cell would rise against her wishes and attune itself exclusively to his will, so quickly, so irrevocably and so totally?

Contrary to all her training, she is his to take, just as he pleases – and it pleases him to explore her slowly, until she is truly his creature. Panting, wild-eyed and shameless, she tears open her bodice and offers up her pink-tipped breasts and alabaster neck.

He moves swiftly, and his mouth is almost upon her when they are interrupted. Fangs bared and bloodlust in his eyes, he drops her and turns to face his attacker, but for him it is already too late. A sharp wooden stake has found its mark and his heart is stilled – forever.

"Not quite to plan," Martin admits to his dishevelled sister, Constance, as he helps her to her feet, "but a successful out-come, nevertheless."

She adjusts her clothing. Relentless vampire killers, they are ready to resume the hunt.

# MOTHER

On Easter Sunday, I consider God's children gathering in the cool hush of a great cathedral where marble columns rise like giant tree trunks supporting a vaulted canopy of stone. In the immense nave, watched over by sculpted angels and saints assembled in shiny segments set high in stained-glass windows, they wait in awe for a cardinal to deliver his sermon.

"From the Book of John, Verse 6.40," he begins, drawing on the two-thousand-year-old wisdom of the Bible, "For it is the will of my Father that everyone who looks on the Son and believes in him should have eternal life, and I will raise him up."

His deep voice fortified with the power of his God-given authority, the Cardinal speaks of the miraculous raising of Lazarus, of Christ's resurrection and his ascension to Heaven. He unites his flock in hope and leads it in a prayer of thanks to the Heavenly Father for His gift of eternal life.

My sermon is birdsong and my wisdom predates religion. My holy book is the Periodic Table and my miracles are recorded in DNA. I have no need for stone edifices for I am one with stone and I am everywhere. Men dream of a Heavenly father to assuage their fear of dying, but in the end they return to me, their Mother. Ashes to ashes and dust to dust.

# TAMING TOMMY

Tommy has his faults. For starters, he's a very naughty boy. Just ask any girl who's ever had the end of her pony tail dipped in a pot of paint or glue when she's been unlucky enough to sit in front of him during art class. He's neither well-organised nor clever, but just ask anyone and they'll tell you that Tommy's the funniest boy in our class. He cracks us up, pulling silly faces when our teacher, Mrs Flanagan, isn't looking, or singing out of tune even when she is.

When he bursts into the class this morning, Tommy is wild-eyed and breathless. Not knowing what he's up to this time, we're all ready for a good laugh until we hear him blathering on about a lion in the corridor. Mrs Flanagan's not impressed.

"That's preposterous!" she snaps, striding for the door.

Of course, she doesn't believe him and to be fair, neither would any of us if we didn't know Tommy so well. You see, Tommy may not be perfect, but he always tells the truth. If Tommy says it, then we know that there's a lion out there, but what none of us knows about Mrs Flanagan is that she is descended from a legendary line of lion tamers and is completely unafraid. Brandishing a chair and a metre rule, she confronts the escaped circus lion and takes control until his keepers arrive to recapture him.

It's funny how things turn out. Mrs Flanagan has her faults, but after today, even Tommy agrees that she's the best and bravest teacher in the entire world.

# TWO HEARTS

Deep in the hush of the forest where the buttress roots of a great grandfather tree reach out in endless serpentine coils, she leaves the track, drawn by a bashful patch of wildflowers blushing under a spotlight of sunshine in the gloom. Exploring further afield, she is clambering over a large pile of moss-covered stones when the tread of her hiking boot scuffs the surface of the largest one and exposes some intriguing markings. When she scrapes the stone clean, she is astonished; two hearts, intertwined as one, are painstakingly etched into its surface.

Pulse quickening, she realises the possible significance of her find. Local legend has it that once a noble lady fled into this forest to live in seclusion under the protection of her lover, a handsome knight. The story goes that the lady lies somewhere hereabouts and that her lover guards her still.

Believing that the stones may be a cairn marking the lady's grave, she cannot wait to share the news. Then, with the late afternoon chill gathering around her ankles, she imagines she sees him, the handsome knight, watching her from the shadows. Stepping back in fright, she loses her footing on the slippery ground and falls heavily, snapping her neck. She will be telling no one.

# POSTULANTS

I raise one shapely eyebrow and stand back from the mirror to make a final inspection. My skin is baby-smooth and subtly blushed to accentuate my classic high cheekbones. My eyelashes are seductively full and my eyes, shadowed in smoky tones, are expertly outlined. Pink and plump, my lips look totally kissable and my thick hair parted in the middle, falls in a continuous glossy wave to my tiny waist. I am well pleased with what I see. Face and hair perfect, it's time to dress.

I shiver with pleasure as I slip a shift of finest white silk over my bare shoulders. The elegant simplicity of its design epitomises quality and although I pair it with comfortable leather sandals, I look very much like the goddess I adore. I am ready.

My sisters arrive, similarly groomed, and spirits soaring, we follow the teachings and example set by our spiritual leader, the Venerable Kim Kardashian, Goddess of Unreal Reality. Clutching our Kardashian Holy Pocketbooks, we enter the gleaming, multi-storey Kardashian Temple of Merchandise to pay homage with our KardashiKredit Kards and experience the ritual retail ecstasy of our faith.

In the name of the mother, the daughters and the Holy West Coast, may the dollar be forever with me. Awomen.

# THE PRACTICAL
# PRIOR

The hem of his cassock sweeping a wet trail through the dewy grass, Brother Timothy rushes across the cloister.

"Forgive me, Father," he blurts out, falling to his knees.

I gently help him to his feet.

"Whatever is the matter?" I ask.

Brother Timothy's long face is all the longer for the burden of his worry. He is responsible for the security of our sacristy and he has just discovered its damaged door.

"There has been a theft," he wails, "Our holiest relic is gone."

The relic, a fragment of the Cross of Jesus, not only brings the priory great prestige, but also a generous income from the thousands of pilgrims who visit us every year to see it. Its loss would be a disaster, but I am a practical man. I assure Brother Timothy that our fragment of the Cross of Jesus is safe in my keeping. I tell him how, through the grace of God, I intercepted the thief, a desperate wretch looking for a cure, and blessed him with the forgiveness of our Heavenly Father's love before allowing him to depart.

While the sacristy door is repaired, I gouge another splinter of timber from the underside of my bed. This is not the first time I have had to replace our fragment of the Cross of Jesus with a humble chip of wood, but it is for the greater good and I am confident that God, in all His wisdom, understands.

# TREASURE HUNTER

She is having coffee on the balcony, enjoying the view of the escarpment. When her friend phones, she removes the chunky sapphire earring from her 'listening ear' and puts it on the table where its deep blue heart throbs to life in the morning sunshine. As she chats, she is oblivious to its singular beauty.

Later when she discovers the precious earring missing, she searches everywhere – frantically – beginning with the balcony.

Just beyond the boundary of her Blue Mountains home, in the scrub and well protected by a cover of thick shrubbery, the satin bowerbird admires his new acquisition. His carefully constructed bower is decorated with the treasures he has gathered: bright blue plastic straws and pegs, silky blue feathers, pale blue bottle tops, silvery blue cigarette packs, waxy blue sweet wrappers, shreds of whisper blue paper and the blue perfection of a sapphire earring.

He is never oblivious to the singular beauty of blue.

# MEALS ON WHEELS

Because her phone doesn't charge overnight, its alarm doesn't ring, and she oversleeps. She looks a fright, too, with her dishevelled hair, bags under mascara-caked eyes and a massive pimple crowning the tip of her nose. If it wasn't for an important meeting at work, she would stay at home.

Having missed her usual bus, she drives to work and when she finally arrives, she discovers that on this, the only day since the year dot that she hasn't checked her emails over breakfast, she has missed the one notifying her that the meeting has been cancelled. If things have started off badly, they only get worse.

"Why didn't you call me about the meeting?" she snaps at her colleague, who snaps back that he did – several times – and what is her problem?

A sheepish apology doesn't cut it and the cloud that hangs between them for the rest of the day, makes working together difficult. Though she stays late, she accomplishes little and by the time she leaves she an almighty headache. Her car skids off the road and into a deep gully on her way home.

For her, the crash is best described as the tragic culmination of a long series of unfortunate events. However, for him it is simply serendipity. He cannot stand by and watch her bleed to death, not when he's a hungry vampire.

# GHOST WRITER

Her sleek laptop computer is nothing like the old clunkers on which I learned to type. I doubt she could manage on a sturdy manual typewriter or cope with the endless, fingernail-breaking practice exercises I had to endure. If I typed "Quality not quantity quoted Queenie" once to strengthen my pinkies, I did it a hundred times over. The same applied to "The quick brown fox jumps over the lazy dog". I kept at it until I could accurately hit every letter of the alphabet, every time. Whatever I typed, I persevered until my responses were automatic and my copy was perfect.

As a professional writer, though, learning to touch-type proved to be one of the best decisions I ever made. Sure, equipment has changed since then. Manual typewriters gave way to electric ones and they, in turn, have given way to word processing software and computers, but the configuration of the QWERTY keyboard has remained the same.

Nowadays, my fingers still hover obediently over the home keys of her keyboard, ready to go. However, she doesn't know I'm here with her or that we're sharing a chair. What's more, she thinks the story we're writing is all her own doing. Ha! As if one so young, who picks and pecks at her keyboard with two fingers, could ever produce such a mature work. It's our story; I'm in her head.

After critics laud her debut novel, as I'm sure they will, I'll come up with a sequel for her. However, I must say, writing was much easier for me when I was alive.

*Note: The home keys on a QWERTY keyboard are A S D F (left hand) and J K L ; (right hand). Touch-typists rest their fingers over the home keys. The two keys, G and H, between the right and left home keys often have a raised dot or line so that touch-typists can relocate their fingers on a keyboard without needing to look at the keys.*

# ONCE UPON A TIME

# MEN OF THE CLOTH

Byzantine monks, Gregorius and Nicolaus are nearly home. They have been across the Black Sea, the Caucasus Mountains, along the northern edge of the Gobi Desert and all the way to China and back. As men of the cloth, they have enjoyed the regular hospitality and protection of Silk Road traders, travelling on camels in guarded caravans, buying and selling their luxury goods – bales of precious silk, fine horses and valuable spices – at town bazaars along the way. However, on the last leg of their journey, Gregorius and Nicolaus must walk alone, an old horse carrying their few possessions, and on the outskirts of Constantinople, thieves jump out from behind a rocky outcrop and bar their way.

The monks' faces harden, and their hands tighten around their stout bamboo walking canes as they watch the thieves rifling through the baskets and bags on their horse. The search reveals nothing of value, but monks have a reputation as wily operators and the thieves are no respecters of the dignity of the cloth. They look under the monk's grizzled beards and shake out their dusty cassocks. Gregorius and Nicolaus are poked and prodded, but when they leave, the thieves are empty handed – and the Byzantine emperor's hidden treasure is safe.

Their secret mission completed, Gregorius and Nicolaus proudly present their humble bamboo walking canes to Justinian

I, Emperor of Byzantium, at the Great Palace of Constantinople. Each stick is packed with precious silkworm eggs smuggled out of China. Justinian has grand plans for them.

*Note: In Byzantium, wearing silk was a luxury reserved for royalty. However, appetite for the luxurious cloth was insatiable, not only in Byzantium, but also across mainland Europe. Silk was imported into Constantinople, the capital of Byzantium, but supply was strictly controlled by Persia and it never kept up with demand. In 553 AD, Justinian I, Emperor of Byzantium, sent Imperial monks on a secret mission to China (nearly 7000 kilometres away) to bring back enough silkworms to establish a silk industry in Constantinople. The industry thrived, and Byzantium soon monopolised the supply of silk to Europe.*

# RICHES

She wasn't just a girl, like me. She was a princess, a precious jewel that dazzled as she passed me by. The embodiment of everything I desired, she rode in elegant carriages, dressed in the finest brocades and silk, ate candied violets and slept on a feather bed.

"Don't be envious of her, little one," Papa used to tell me when he saw the longing in my eyes. "You will have riches she can only dream about."

I would smile to make him happy, but I never believed him.

After her marriage in a faraway land, the princess is now a queen, visiting home with her elderly, foreign husband, her king, at her side and as their open carriage passes by, I am shocked by what I see. Though she is wrapped in ermine, the princess – now a queen – looks so sad and when the old man, her husband and king, leans close to whisper in her ear, she turns away, repulsed. It is then, in that moment, that I understand that Papa was right.

"Come, Mama," my small daughter calls, beckoning me to join her.

Her father, my handsome young husband, is striding towards me, carrying her on his broad shoulders and as I reach up to kiss them, I realise that they are the embodiment of all the riches I desire.

*Note: In the Middle Ages, princesses or high-ranking girls were used to forge alliances between powerful families, kingdoms and principalities. Promised in marriage at an early age, the primary role of princesses or young queens was to produce male heirs for their husbands. Their marriages involved the bride leaving home to live in distant kingdoms or principalities, often never to return home again.*

# ROYAL BLOOD

The long minutes have inched into interminable hours. Surrounded by a thick hush of pinched faces, Anne is at Henry's bedside. Her dainty hands clutch her prayer book and her head is elegantly bowed as she prays for Henry to regain his senses. She need not look up to know that all eyes are on him. Unconscious, Henry still dominates the room. His leg wound is serious enough, but he has suffered such a blow to his head as would kill any other man. Henry is not any other man; he is the King of England and she is Anne, his queen. She needs him to live.

As if it is a talisman, Anne touches the B-shaped pendant that embellishes her exquisite pearl necklace. A gleaming gold B for Boleyn, it reminds her of what is important. She is with child again and this time she is certain she is carrying a boy. Henry will have his heir. He will love her again and Boleyn blood will flow through the veins of the future kings of England. Her position as the most powerful woman in the kingdom will be secure. Henry must survive.

In her prayers, Anne begs and cajoles for Henry's recovery and when he rouses, she rejoices. Eager to be the first face he sees, Anne leans in close, but as Henry opens his eyes, she is gripped by a familiar and utterly terrifying sensation. All is lost. She has started to bleed.

*Note: On 24 January 1536, King Henry VIII of England suffered a serious head injury while jousting at Greenwich Palace. Days later, on 29 January, his wife, Queen Anne (Boleyn), suffered the miscarriage (a male child, according to Eustace Chapuys, the Imperial Ambassador, who reported Anne Boleyn's miscarriage in a dispatch to Emperor Charles V). Although Henry recovered from the prolonged period of unconsciousness that followed his accident, historians speculate that he may have suffered brain damage that affected his personality and moods. In some part at least, this may contribute to understanding why Anne Boleyn was executed a few short months later on 19 May 1536.*

# IRRECONCILABLE
# DIFFERENCES

They marry in haste and have unrealistic expectations of each other. She thinks he will always be her brave prince, her hero, and he thinks she will always be his rescued princess, his glittering prize, but the honeymoon ends quickly. Having spent much of her adolescence alone, she soon finds she prefers her own company while he, on the other hand, would rather be with his bobble-headed sycophants – especially the pretty ones.

Their marriage doomed, she knows he wants to be rid of her. However, considering her background, cutting her hair and banishing her to the tower keep seems unnecessarily harsh. No matter how she screams and rages, she knows that nobody will come to her aid. Rapunzel is pragmatic, though, and remains calm. She knows her hair will grow again and in the meantime, she will watch the world from her window and enjoy her beloved books in peace.

*Note: Although Rapunzel is best known as a German fairy tale first published by the Brothers Grimm in 1812, it is an adaptation of a French fairy tale with the same title that appeared in the late 1700s. Rapunzel also resembles an 11th century Persian tale called Rubada. Some elements of Rapunzel may have originated from accounts of Saint Barbara, who the story goes, was locked in a tower by her father.*

# A COUNTRY PRACTICE

The village doctor deals with all manner of injuries and illnesses, but his patients this morning, a husband and wife, present him with an unusual challenge. Whilst they live under the same roof and eat at the same table, the husband is wasting away while his wife grows as round as a ball.

"What's wrong with us, doc?" the husband wants to know, his eyes huge in his cavernous face.

A physical examination confirms what the doctor suspects. Despite their vastly different body weights, both patients are malnourished. They cannot be eating properly.

Her chins wobbling like pink blancmange when she speaks, the wife is indignant.

"But how can that be when we have all that we want?" she wants to know.

Nodding in agreement, her husband adds, "We feast on meat. I eat no fat. She eats no lean and between us, we lick the platter clean."

The doctor is recommending a flexible diet, one that includes greens and grains, when his nurse bursts into the room.

"There's an emergency at Gloucester!" she cries.

Jack Sprat and his wife's dietary problems must wait.

"An old woman has just eaten a fly, a spider, a bird, a cat, a dog, a goat, a cow and a horse and perhaps she'll die!"

Doctor Foster grabs his bag and umbrella and rushes out into the rain.

*Note: Jack Sprat first appeared in 1639 in a collection of English proverbs. There are many theories about the character of Jack Sprat – from King Charles I to Robin Hood – but none are proven. The traditional rhymes/songs referenced are:*

*Jack Sprat could eat no fat.*
*His wife could eat no lean.*
*And so between them both, you see,*
*They licked the platter clean.*

*There was an old woman who swallowed a fly.*
*I don't know why she swallowed a fly.*
*Perhaps, she'll die ... and so on and so on.*

*Doctor Foster went to Gloucester*
*In a shower of rain;*
*He stepped in a puddle,*
*Right up to his middle,*
*And never went there again.*

# MOSQUITO

At twenty-one, Horatio is already a British naval captain. For three long months, he has sailed the 28-gun HMS Hinchinbrook up the San Juan River, through infernally hot and mosquito-ridden jungle, to reach and capture Granada, but Spanish resistance along the way has been fierce and with the coming of the wet season, the campaign seems doomed. Supplies and ammunition are running as low as the spirits of all on board.

In the privacy of his quarters, Horatio shrugs off his frock coat, loosens his shirt and prepares to read the weekly despatches. He is light-headed and has neither taste nor energy for the task, but there is splendid news in the satchel. He has a new commission – a promotion. He is ordered to take command of a powerful warship, a 44 gunner, the HMS Janus!

With that, Horatio lies on his bed, intent on halting the progression of an emerging headache and to contemplate his future. He is finding it increasingly hard to concentrate, but he quickly associates the name of his new command with Janus, the Roman God of beginnings and concludes, as he slips into a fevered sleep, that the HMS Janus is an omen of great things to come.

However, the Roman God Janus has two faces. While one face looks to the future, the other looks to the past and since arriving in Nicaragua, Horatio has been infected by a malaria-carrying mosquito.

He is going nowhere.

*Note: In 1780, during the American War of Independence, Horatio Nelson, who is celebrated for his later defeat of Napoleon at Waterloo, participated in the ill-fated San Juan Expedition, which aimed to capture Granada and Leon for the British. The campaign was a failure. Dysentery and malaria cut a swath through the British forces. Due to a serious and protracted bout of malaria, Nelson never took command of the HMS Janus.*

# NO ESCAPE

Their grand escape has become a desperate struggle for survival. Though they planned carefully, somehow the children, brother and sister, are lost. On this, their third day without food or shelter, they huddle together, shivering in clammy clothes, the damp ground leeching the warmth from their skinny bones.

"We must get moving," the brother tells his sister, as he helps her to her feet.

Afternoon is slipping into evening when the starving children smell something cooking nearby. Mad with hunger, they are oblivious to the thorns and prickles that claw at them and scratch as they push their way through the undergrowth. Expecting to find a campfire, instead they find a cottage, nestled amongst the trees, smoke curling lazily from its chimney.

The sister hesitates. Who would live out here, all alone?

"What about the gypsies?" she asks, clinging to her brother's arm.

He dismisses her concern. He's heard there's a murderous band of gypsies with a hideaway in the woods, too, but he is dubious.

"Don't be silly," he scoffs. "That's just a story parents tell to keep children away from the woods."

Reassured, but still uncertain, she is so relieved when the old lady answers their knock.

"Oh my!" the old lady exclaims, finding the two waifs on her doorstep.

Gathering Hansel and Gretel in her arms, she quickly ushers them inside and surreptitiously locks the door.

*Note: Stories of abandoned children like Hansel and Gretel may have originated in the Middle Ages during the Great Famine 1315-1351. The best-known version of Hansel and Gretel appeared in* Children's and Household Tales *by Brothers Grimm in 1812. In that version, both parents agreed to send the children into the woods, rather than a wicked stepmother who features in contemporary versions of the story.*

# CHILDHOOD LOST

As a child I spent my summer holidays in this beautiful place with the family and friends who populate my memories in inflatable swimming tubes, water wings, sunhats, swimsuits and stripy beach towels. Now, after many years I have returned and as I contemplate the sparkling Mediterranean from the balcony of my resort hotel, the afternoon sea breeze playing gently with my hair, I discover the white caps still dance on the same waves and the air still leaves the same sea-salty kiss on my lips, but the once crowded beach is empty – no bathers, no picnickers, no joggers, no beachcombers, no one.

We used to comb the beach at low tide, searching for treasures given up by the sea: spiralling seashells, twisted driftwood and the occasional curio, such as the porcelain tea cup my brother once found. Perhaps, this is how it always is in autumn after the holiday makers have gone, but I doubt it.

Nothing is the same in Bodrum.

Later, as the light fades to mournful grey, I say a prayer for the tiny boy washed up on the beach today and mourn childhood lost.

*Note: An image of the body of Syrian toddler Aylan Kurdi, a refugee, whose body was washed up on the beach at Bodrum in 2015, became a symbol of the unprecedented refugee crisis of the times.*

# IT TAKES
# A VILLAGE

Despite the heavy cloak wrapped around her gaunt frame, she shivers as she glances at the barometer on the wall. The mercury has been dropping all afternoon and the wind whipping at the shutters confirms the heavy weather outside. From the safety of the cottage, high on the cliff, she can hear the breakers smashing onto the rocks below. This is a wild, black night for seafarers. Her men, her husband and sons, are out in it and all she can do is pace the floor, praying for the souls of those who are caught in this storm – for those who will perish in it and, especially, for those who will come home.

Grim-faced, her husband and sons return, and all are safely abed when roused at dawn by hammering on their door. A ship has foundered in the cove. Lives have been lost and the wreck has been looted.

"Stand aside, Missus," the excise men demand, and the family knows better than to resist.

Their home is ransacked in a search for the stolen goods. In this Cornish village of pinched cheeks and hollow eyes, where the tin mines have closed, and men have no work, no one is beyond suspicion, but the excise men leave empty-handed. They are no match for a community united against them. The haul is safely hidden and tomorrow the children will have food.

*Note: During the 1800s, many families living in Cornwall, England, were reliant on mining for their income. They experienced protracted periods of hardship. When employment was insecure and food too expensive, some men turned in desperation to smuggling and plundering ships that were wrecked along the coast after straying or being lured into dangerous waters.*

# THE PARSON'S DAUGHTER

While Father works on his next sermon in the study, I embroider in the adjoining room, but no more pretty needlework, all flowers and curlicues, for me. Instead, I am embroidering the fabric of my imagination and with my very boldest threads of thought. Father draws both comfort and strength from the Bible that is always by his side, but not I. Though we are close by, Father knows little, how far we are apart.

If Father were to join me on the settee by the drawing room window, he may notice my heightened colour and the twinkle in my eye as I gaze past the village to the endless moors beyond, but he would not connect the two. Nor would he suspect the passionate scene that pulses, wild and wicked, through my veins: windswept lovers, devouring and sustaining each other in equal measure. Untamed and untameable, they inhabit a darker part of Yorkshire's soul and though I hide it well enough, they also inhabit me.

We face each other across the table at lunch, Father and me. He knows me as Emily Brontë, his gentle daughter, but I am Heathcliff and I am Catherine Earnshaw, too, and I have such a tale to tell as would fill a book.

*Note: Heathcliff and Catherine Earnshaw are characters from* Wuthering Heights. *First published in 1847,* Wuthering Heights *was Emily Brontë's first and only novel. She died from tuberculosis one year later at the age of twenty-nine. Her father, the Reverend Patrick Brontë outlived his six children and died in 1861 at the age of 84. "I am Heathcliff" is arguably one of the most recognisable, discussed and analysed quotes of all time.*

# THE GOVERNOR'S WIFE

When her maid taps at her door, Adelaide is already awake. This will be her first Christmas in the new house and she has a busy day ahead. Before breakfast she will attend Christmas Mass with her husband and later they will host a banquet for dignitaries and their wives. Befitting her husband's high office, Adelaide understands that she must look her very best. She will wear a dusky rose dress of the finest silk, tailored in the latest style, with matching jacket and bonnet.

Adelaide slips into her undergarments, calf length drawers and a cotton chemise before enjoying a leisurely stretch, a freedom she must surrender as her maid laces her firmly into her whalebone corset. An elegantly embroidered camisole covers her corset and then Adelaide steps into her six petticoats, the first a delicate under petticoat, the remainder stiffly starched and heavily flounced to give her outfit the modish fullness that everyone admires. The shimmering dress and jacket are next, followed by white gloves and dainty boots. Finally, her maid positions Adelaide's beribboned bonnet over her fashionably low bun.

Although December is high summer in the southern hemisphere, and despite Sydney's dreadful heat, insufferable blowflies and the myriad inconveniences of colonial life, Adelaide is stoically resplendent in her Christmas finery. On her husband's arm, she is every inch the ideal Victorian wife.

*Note: Adelaide Annabella Tuite Dalton, stepdaughter of the Marquess of Headfort married Sir John Young in 1835. She travelled to Sydney when her husband was appointed Governor of New South Wales in 1861. They remained in Australia for six years.*

# STITCH

Needle in. Needle out. Needle in. Needle out.

Polly looks up from her needlework to watch a fly as it bumbles against a window pane. They are both trapped, Polly and the fly, inside her stuffy school room on the second floor of the fine country home in which Polly and her family live.

From her small desk, Polly can hear cicadas drumming and her older brothers laughing as they bat a ball around on the lawn outside. Home for school holidays, and beyond the jurisdiction of Miss Rose, the governess, they are free to play.

Miss Rose approaches Polly in a cloud of lavender scent, her skirts swishing softly across the timber floor.

She casts her critical eye over Polly's cross stitching, checking that it is neither too loose, nor too tight, evenly spaced and accurately positioned in straight rows.

"Stop daydreaming, Polly and attend to your sewing," she chides her young pupil.

Polly is making slow progress on her cross-stitch sampler. She sets aside her embroidery, which is stretched tightly across a wooden frame, to rethread her needle with a different coloured cotton thread. She has just finished the last cross stitch on "H", the first letter in the word "HOME", which along with a cottage and garden, is part of her needlework's design. Polly hates the monotony of sewing.

Needle in. Needle out. Needle in. Needle out.

"Remember, Polly, that a fine sewing stitch is the hallmark of an accomplished gentlewoman," Miss Rose reminds her for the umpteenth time, but Polly frowns crossly.

She wishes that her brothers had to stay inside and sew, and that accomplished gentleman had to stay home to look after them, while she travels the world with accomplished gentle-women having adventures and making grand discoveries. She toys with the idea of embroidering the word "HELP" instead of "HOME". However, Miss Rose takes needlework very seriously and Polly knows that she would only make her unpick the stitches and start again.

The fly is still bumbling. The cicadas are still drumming. Polly's brothers are still playing – and Polly has a plan.

While Miss Rose is carefully dipping her quill pen in and out of the inkpot and writing elegant words in her journal, Polly quietly sabotages her needlework with pinched stitches and a hopelessly tangled thread.

"I think I've done something wrong," she announces when Miss Rose is carefully rolling the ink blotter over her work.

As Miss Rose bends over Polly's cross stitch sampler, tutting and grumbling, Polly opens the window and liberates the fly.

"I'm afraid this will take a while to fix, Polly," Miss Rose concludes and directs Polly to go and find some flowers for them to press later in the day.

Polly is out of the door before Miss Rose can change her mind. Free at last, she whoops and runs amongst the daisies until she collapses with a pain in her side, a stitch, her kind of stitch, not the kind that is the hallmark of an accomplished gentle-woman.

Flat on her back, sun on her freckled face, Polly knows just what to do about it.

Breathe in. Breathe out. Breathe in. Breathe out.

Smile.

*Note: In Australia in the early 1800s, wealthy parents employed a governess to teach their daughters a range of subjects such as reading, penmanship, geography, history, singing, piano, drawing and needlework. While governesses also provided lessons for the sons of wealthy parents, boys were sent to school when they turned eight. The importance of a formal education for boys was recognised, but genteel society saw little need to offer the same opportunity to girls, whose fortunes relied primarily on their marriageability.*

# SPARROWS

As he waits for the music to begin, the old man on the park bench watches the passing parade. After a harsh winter, Londoners have emerged from the gloom and are soaking up the spring sunshine. Fine ladies with parasols float by on clouds of pastel silk and taffeta, accompanied by gentleman companions in expensive, pin-striped promenade suits.

A crowd forms around the bandstand. The lure of an open-air concert is irresistible and as the performance begins, the old man sits quietly, following the antics of some children. He smiles to himself, envying their youthful agility. They elbow their way between the concert-goers, darting in and around like hungry sparrows and if they are noticed at all, they are ignored and deemed unworthy of attention.

Though the afternoon is warm, the old man gathers his oversized coat around him. His bones are stiff from being still for too long and he is ready to move on. By the time he leaves Hyde Park by the Apsley Gate, he has acquired a coterie of scruffy looking children, all vying for his attention.

"Easy pickings, Mr Fagin," one says, but the old man silences him with a glare.

They are still in public and it is not the time to brag about their stolen goods.

*Note: Fagin is a character in* Oliver Twist, *a novel by Charles Dickens, published in 1838. A receiver of stolen goods, Fagin manages a group of street urchins who he trains to pick pockets for him. Charles Dickens' novels expose the underbelly of Victorian England, and in particular, the perilous existence of the poor and homeless.*

# WORK AND PLAY

At closing time, the boy scrapes and washes the scored surface of the butcher's block and sweeps the floor, removing the sawdust, clotted and clumpy with gore, before replacing it with fresh. The butcher, his apron stiff with blood, scours his cleaver and knives before sluicing his face and arms with cold water. They've done a brisk trade and he is feeling generous.

"Here lad," he says, giving the boy a paper-wrapped parcel to take home.

In the package is a bullock's tongue, plump and pink, a piece of boiling beef and a fat slice of lard.

"Thanks, Mr Jack!" the boy cries and clutching his prize to his skinny chest, he rushes off, disappearing into the heavy fog.

After chopping, slicing, filleting, boning, mincing and grinding his way through a mountain of meat and offal, the butcher has done more than enough work and he is itching to play.

As always, he finds a willing playmate in the rat-infested alleys of Whitechapel. Teeth chattering in the bitter cold, she is lifting her filthy skirts when she catches a glimpse of the butcher's knife, a razor sharp six-inch blade – but it is already too late.

While London sleeps, the butcher makes a fresh batch of his premium sausages and his grizzly game concludes.

*Note: Jack the Ripper is the name given to a serial killer whose gruesome murders terrorized Londoners in the 1880s. Active around the Whitechapel district of London, Jack mutilated his female victims in a way that suggested he had knowledge and prowess with anatomy. Jack the Ripper was never caught. His identity remains unknown, but perhaps, he was a butcher.*

# GETTING IT RIGHT

He recognises her in the corridor. She lives in his electorate. Small in stature and clothed in modest browns and drab greys, in this company Mrs Kirk is a sparrow among strutting roosters. Yet he understands that this fragile creature is also an inspirational steward of the Women's Christian Temperance Union and a tireless supporter of the wretched souls at the Elizabeth Frye Retreat for wayward women. He is intrigued, but with the sitting about to begin, he must join the surge of other parliamentarians heading for the chamber.

When Mrs Kirk suddenly materialises at his side, he protects her, instinctively using his arms to shield her from the crowd.

"Can I rely on you?" she implores him as he gently shepherds her to the side.

This is an important day for her, the culmination of many months of dedicated effort.

"I will always do what is right, my dear," he promises.

From his seat in the chamber, he can see Mrs Kirk and her supporters in the public gallery. They have reason to be hopeful. The Victorian government has already granted married women the right to own property and to attend university, but what they want now is a step too far. He will do what is right. The very notion of women voting is against the natural order.

Despite the Women's Suffrage Petition of 1891 having

thirty thousand signatures, he is instrumental in voting it down.

*Note: Maria Elizabeth Kirk (1855-1929), a temperance advocate and social reformer, organised and presented to the Victorian parliament a huge petition for women's enfranchisement in 1891. Sometimes referred to as the Monster Petition, it contains some thirty thousand signatures of women from all walks of life. The signatures were collected door-to-door and on the streets. The original petition is approximately 260 metres long and 200mm wide and is made of paper pasted to cotton or linen fabric backing, rolled onto a cardboard spindle.*

# TOUGH LOVE

The day is bright and sunny, but all is not well.

She knows she shouldn't hang about all day worrying about him, but she is his mother and she cannot help herself. Rain or shine, he's never at home anymore and she wouldn't mind if he was out doing something useful, something low-key that doesn't attract an audience. Instead, he is infatuated with fame and his mother fears that his attention-seeking will end badly.

In the beginning, she'd held hopes that he was just going through a bit of a phase and that he might grow out of it, but if anything, his dramatic tendencies have just become stronger. Now she has had enough of it. Tonight, when he comes home for dinner, she is going to put one of her feet down and things are going to change.

There'll be no more endlessly climbing up and down the water spout for the amusement of the world's children. Children everywhere are going to have to find something else to sing about because, as of tomorrow, Incy Wincy Spider is grounded!

*Note: First appearing at the beginning of the 20th Century, Incy Wincy (or Istsy Bitsy) Spider, is a relatively modern inclusion to our most popular nursery rhyme and songs. The words are:*
*Incy Wincy Spider climbed up the water spout*
*Down came the rain and washed poor Incy out*

*Out came the sunshine and dried up all the rain*
*So Incy Wincy Spider climbed up the spout again.*

# ICON

Fastidious about her appearance, she dips into her handbag, taking a moment to powder her nose and refresh her lipstick before leaving the plane. From her perfectly positioned pillbox hat to the polished tops of her pumps, her look is flawless. A blush pink bouclé, her classic suit has a fitted knee length skirt and double-breasted Chanel jacket with a contrasting navy-blue collar and piping along its cuffs and the tops of its pockets. Underneath it, she is wearing a sleeveless, navy blue, silk blouse. Satisfied that she is looking her very best, she pulls on her white kid gloves and steps out into the sunshine with her husband.

Cheering crowds line the streets to catch a glimpse of them, smiling and waving from their open limousine as they make their way to a lunchtime speaking engagement. They are America's golden couple, President Kennedy and his beautiful wife, Jackie, and they are a moment away from chaos.

Shots ring out. Her husband fatally wounded, Jackie cradles his head in her lap. Her exquisite blush pink bouclé ensemble turns blood red and just like that, the 35th President of the United States, husband to Jackie and father to John and Caroline, is dead. Though continually urged to do so, Jackie declines to change out of her bloodied clothes and she knows best. For the remainder of the day, she will wear her loss for all to see and, as always, her instincts are impeccable.

*Note: Jackie Kennedy's iconic bouclé ensemble, still caked with her husband's blood, is now stored in a custom-made acid-free box in the climate-controlled National Archives building in College Park, Maryland along with assassin, Lee Harvey Oswald's rifle, bullets and bullet fragments from the shooting, the original windshield of the limousine, and more than five million pages of assassination-related records.*

# PREDATOR

A large Kalahari lion in peak condition, Xanda is attended by two adult lionesses. His velvety nose wrinkling each time he licks his massive paw to fastidiously wipe himself clean, he spends the afternoon grooming himself. Several cubs play nearby. Secure under his protection, they are unperturbed by the latent danger posed by their proximity to their father's powerful jaws – jaws that can snap a wildebeest's neck or strangle it to death. Instead, the cubs nuzzle into his handsome mane and attack the black tuft at the end of his tail whenever it flicks in their direction.

His tawny coat rippling gold in the sunshine, Xanda swaggers down to the waterhole where highly-strung impalas, waterbucks and zebras startle and scatter on his approach. In these parts, Xanda is king, his authority imposed with enormous canine teeth and deadly retractable claws. Animals tremble at his roar, but today Xanda has a full belly from an earlier kill so he is soft-pawed and gentle.

As he is returning to the pride, Xanda is felled by a single shot. For all his magnificence, even a mighty lion king is no match for a cashed-up trophy hunter armed with a long-range rifle.

*Note: The son of Cecil, the lion famously killed by a wealthy trophy hunter in Zimbabwe in 2015, Xanda met the same fate on 7 July 2017. Too sad.*

# ENDINGS

# IT'S OVER

Standing by the window, she contemplates the spreading bruise of a new day, unaware he is behind her until he speaks.

"Where have you put my car keys?" he asks.

The question is a simple one, but his breath, angry puffs on the exposed skin of her neck, belies the pleasant tone of his voice and she is warned. She must think before she replies. Nothing's ever straightforward where he's concerned. With him, nothing's ever as it seems, and her thoughts are racing. She must find the right answer, quickly. God forbid that he should have to repeat himself.

She knows where his keys are. They're on the coffee table where he left them – and he knows it, too. She hasn't put his keys anywhere. His real intention is to make it clear that he's found her lacking. In this house, she's responsible for keeping everything in its proper place and she hasn't put his keys back where they belong. So, he's not really looking for an answer, but an apology and a promise that it won't happen again.

As she opens her mouth to speak, he raises his hand and she flinches, but he doesn't strike her. Instead, he is gentle.

"Hush," he croons, planting a soft kiss on her blackened eyelid. "We'll discuss this later, when I come home."

So, this is his game. She is supposed to wait and worry all day about what he has in mind for her. Well, not this time. This time she's leaving before he has a chance to stop her.

Within the hour, she is packed, out of the front door and on her way, but nothing is ever as it seems where he's concerned. He knows her well. He's been waiting for her on the corner and now he's ready to play.

Now she waits. What else can she do?

She waits, until night time when, at last, he makes his move.

Bare-footed on the cool marble floor, he pads into their room. Every nerve in her body is screaming. He's been drinking and when he wraps his arms around her and holds her close, his lips whispering his longing across her shoulder blades, she must force herself to smile and lean back into his embrace. Tenderly, terrifyingly so, he twines her long hair around and through his fingers, but she is not easily persuaded, not for an instant. She knows how love and hate coexist and how gentle hands can turn into fists, pumping with rage, or fingers tighten into steel bands around a woman's neck to squeeze the fight out of her.

She closes her eyes and wills herself to relax, but her dread of what will happen next bleeds across the edge of her consciousness. When he kisses her, the sour smell of alcohol on his breathe sickens her and yet she responds affectionately. She has no alternative. If he crushes her beneath him as he penetrates her, it is not the worst thing that can happen. Anything is better than a beating, but she is not spared. When he's finished violating her, he ups the ante.

"Go get me another bottle," he orders her, waving an empty whiskey bottle in her face.

There isn't another bottle of whiskey and she's in trouble. Not anticipating his needs, or catering for them, is a punishable offence. They both know it, and he has her by the arm before she can escape his fury.

A tear rolls down her cheek when she catches a glimpse of her reflection in the small mirror on the sun visor as she drives to the bottle shop. She is still as pretty as a picture – an abstract one with facial features rearranged and peculiarly off-centre. Her broken nose is crooked, and her right eye nestles oddly in its broken eye socket, sitting lower than her left. Her mouth skews downwards, anchored to the end of a jagged scar that runs diagonally from her ear through her cheek to her chin. Smiling is impossible.

She has always blamed herself for the beatings – she somehow triggers the violence – but the truth is that he cannot control his demons and he punishes her for his weakness. She is sure of that now and she'll never get away.

Their car hugs the corners of the deserted road. She is driving at breakneck speed as he dozes in the passenger seat beside her. He is as handsome as ever, but she knows they are the same, both damaged beyond repair. When she drives their car over the cliff, he barely stirs and she is smiling – on the inside.

# NIGHTFALL

Though many years have passed since she lived at Lavender Farm, it enchants her now no less than it did when she was young enough to still believe in faeries. Perhaps she should know better, but she sits quietly and watches, still hoping to see them, the faeries, flitting through the lavender in rippling waves of lilac and pink.

Rejuvenated by the scent of lavender crushed underfoot, she would stay forever, but the sharp-tongued harpies do not appreciate the beauty. They are only concerned about the mess.

"Who's going to clean this up?" they shriek, flapping with indignation.

They don't let her explain and as she clings stubbornly to the lavender, they overpower her. She is quietly sobbing as they wrench her away.

Later – much later perhaps – she wakes, but she is so tired.

The harpies have their ways.

"The nurses tell me you slipped away to do a bit of painting on the craft room walls this morning, Mum," someone, a man, is saying.

His voice is warm like milk chocolate and he kisses her cheek.

Who is he?

As the stranger talks about this and that, there comes a precious moment of clarity when she holds out the handful of lavender she managed to bring back earlier in the day.

"Goodbye, my darling boy," she whispers, a mother to her only son, "I love you."

The setting sun melts red-gold over the plush, purplish fields of lavender and she must hurry home before night falls.

# ANOTHER COUNTRY

One of four sons and the second youngest of eleven children, my uncle died last week. He was the last of them. The others, my dear mother included, all left before him and I find myself remembering them at my grandparents' house. Such a place it was, full of people and always smelling of coffee and cinnamon – or so it seems to me, looking back.

Coming to Australia in the 1950s, my grandparents, Opa and Oma, brought some of Holland with them: decorative pairs of clogs to hang on the walls, windmills and tulips in paintings and prints, carpet runners for the tables and a collection of miniature Amsterdam canal houses, an entire street of them, that found a home on the oak sideboard in the sitting room. We were not allowed to touch them, but sometimes when nobody was looking, I would stand on the sofa and do it anyway. Oma had real chocolate hail for our sandwiches, too – not the crunchy chocolate-flavoured sprinkles used to decorate cakes nowadays, but mounds of scrumptious little logs, one hundred percent Dutch chocolate, the kind that melts on your tongue.

I didn't attend my uncle's funeral; our families have been estranged for many years, but I will always remember him as the young Dutchman at my grandparents' house, the one who clowned around, making us laugh and I am sorry that I didn't know him better.

# THE WAY HOME

Invigorated by the pristine air, he sets out to explore the countryside. On his way back, he stumbles and smashes his head against the jagged edge of a protruding rock. Heavy snow falls, soon tucking him under a wintery blanket as he lies on the ground, unconscious and bleeding from a wound on his temple.

Night descends quickly and the white world flips to black. The power is out, and she is worried sick. He has not answered his phone for hours and she can see nothing past the snowflakes that swirl and churn against the icy window pane. Her fingers tremble as she lights a candle and sets it on the windowsill. She wills its singular flame to show him the way.

He stirs and though it makes no sense to him, he is warm and cosy in his slushy bed. He can barely lift his head, but he feels no pain and when he spots the candlelight, a tiny jewel winking in the vast, velvety night, he remembers her. He knows she is waiting, but there is another light, a much brighter one at the end of a tunnel and loved ones, long since passed, are calling.

She sleeps. The candle burns on, but he is gone.

# FIRST LOVE

They have been together for fifteen years and he still remembers the thrill of seeing her for the first time. He knew instantly that he had to have her, no matter what. She had the looks. She had the class and her body was perfect, but only later when they were alone together, did he realise that it was the way that she responded, almost intuitively, to his touch that set her apart from all others. No matter where he wanted to go or when, she was always ready, too – and they went places he had never been before. She has never let him down.

He sighs. Raking through these memories only makes his decision harder, but it must be made. Things have changed. His needs have changed, and it is time to move on.

He lingers over the photos he has just taken of her. He is not as trim as he used to be, but she has not changed a bit. She is still gorgeous.

With some reluctance, he fills out her details, nominates the price he wants and uploads the photos on the car sales site. Now that he is married and has a child on the way, he needs a family car, but he will never forget his first love.

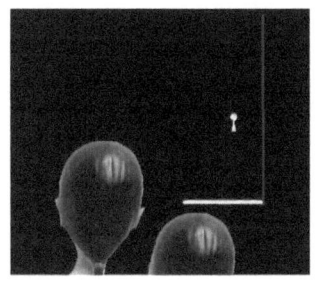

# MIDNIGHT FEAST

"You want a fairy tale?" she snarls through their locked bedroom door. "Here you go. Once upon a time, they lived happily ever after. Now, shut up and go to sleep – or else."

Of course, we know much better than to ask our stepmother for anything, let alone for a bedtime story. We want our Papa, but he is safely out of earshot and she silences us in her usual spiteful way. "Or else" means we will get no breakfast and because we've had no lunch or dinner, either, the very mention of food sets our empty stomachs rumbling.

From our darkened bedroom, we can hear our stepmother cooing in Papa's ear and the smell of the delicious supper they're sharing drives us mad with longing. Afterwards they drink too much wine and as they laugh themselves silly, our resolve hardens. By the time their slack-jawed snores signal they are in bed, we are decided. We climb out of our bedroom window and in through theirs.

Every wicked stepmother deserves wicked stepchildren and it is a simple matter to smother one drunkard with her pillow while the other sleeps on beside her, undisturbed.

Papa will mourn our stepmother for a brief time, but he is fickle. She will be quickly replaced. As we tuck in to our midnight feast, we wonder if we will like her inevitable replacement any better.

# THRESHOLD

She catches a glimpse of him in the dressing table mirror, watching her from the doorway as she brushes her hair, and she smiles. He's always loved her hair. When they were young, he used to tell her that he loved the fiery look of it, the way it flared in the sunshine when she moved. He used to say that he loved the playful feel of it, the tickle against his chin when she rested her head on his shoulder and the scent of it, the lingering essence of her – but all that was so long ago.

Their children say that now he's gone the house is too big for her and that it's time to sell, but they are wrong. They don't understand that he would never leave without her.

Putting the brush aside, she divides her thinning hair into three sections and plaits it. No longer a tumbling mass of youthful promise, it has become a fine cape of silvery wisps, a testament to her long life, she supposes. He said he still loved the look of it, though, the graceful way it framed her face and the gentle way it spoke of their many years together. He said it reminded him of how lucky he had been to grow old at her side.

When she turns out the bedroom light, she senses he is close by and wrapped in her precious memories, she falls asleep straight away.

# ANGEL

I watch her sleeping and I am overwhelmed by my love for her. A ray of sunlight peeps into the darkened room and, for a moment, before I close the gap in the curtain, her hair is a glowing halo on her pillow. She is my precious angel.

Her small hand closes around my thumb as I gently rub her palm. Our breathing is synchronous, deep and slow, and I bask in wonderful memories of her firsts – her first cheeky cherub smile, her first tooth, her first wobbly steps and her first babbled words.

Her skin, so pink and warm to my touch, belies her fragility and the relentless progression of the neurodegenerative disorder that has gradually robbed her of speech, hearing, vision and the ability to move around unassisted. Her paediatrician warns of what is to come.

I lean in close and breathe in her essence, one last time. Then I cover her face with her pillow and release her from the stainless steel and rubber paraphernalia that define her earth-bound existence. Angels must fly free.

# I SPY

With all the commotion next door, the old lady has been expecting them. She's been in her kitchen all morning, preparing some tasty titbits. She loves visitors.

"Do come in, gentlemen," she says when the two policemen arrive at her door just after midday.

Ushering them into her sitting room, she offers them a cup of tea and some lunch. Though pressed for time, neither can resist her invitation. They're both hungry and can easily conduct their interview as they eat.

The freshly baked bread is warm and crusty. The homemade paté is subtlety piquant, the pastries wickedly sweet. However, the officers soon realise that the old lady cannot help them with their enquiries. She can report nothing unusual around the time that her neighbour fell from his ladder the previous night.

"Oh dear," the old lady says when told that the nature of her neighbour's injuries would leave him blind. "He so liked to keep an eye on everyone."

The officers spare her the gory details and, of course, her demeanour doesn't suggest that she already knows, but when they leave, she sets to work, meticulously cleaning her saucepan and blender while her cat eats the last of the paté. With no evidence remaining, she is confident nobody will discover how Peeping Tom lost his eyes or whatever became of them, either.

# THE END OF THE ROAD

Mum's standing at the end of the corridor. Her eyes, the palest of faded blues behind her pink plastic-framed glasses, are troubled by indecision and when I reach her, I take her hand – so small in mine – and give it my warmest everything's-going-to-be-okay squeeze.

"I'm so very sorry, dear," she apologizes, her voice trembling with emotion, "I can't remember where I parked the car."

In this building where each labyrinthine floor looks pretty much the same as the next, I am guessing that many people get confused.

"Done the same thing myself," I reassure her. "And more than once, too."

Being diplomatic comes easily and she's happy to let me take the lead.

"The car's not on this level, Mum," I explain, heading for the lift.

As we glide between floors, Mum straightens her shoulders and smooths her snowy curls. I'm glad she's feeling better, but I hate the way she's shrinking, slipping away from me. Where we used to stand eye-to-eye, nowadays my mother barely reaches my shoulders, but that's not the worst of it.

"Here's the car, right where you left it," I must force myself to say as I reunite her with her hospital bed and she starts fussing around for her car keys.

My heart is breaking: Mum's problem isn't forgetting where her car's parked, but not understanding that she no longer owns one.

# THE TWILIGHT TRAVELLER

Expertly manoeuvring his craft, the gondolier plies his trade gently, propelling us smoothly through the softly lapping waters. Quietly, we slip under the Rialto Bridge and glide past the Bridge of Sighs. For all her beauty, the floating city of Venice is a fragile old lady on shaky legs, ever-threatened by the very water that sustains her, but today she is basking in the sunshine, her stucco palazzos blushing pale pinks and apricots as we pass.

I am trailing my fingers in the tepid warmth of the Grand Canal when, as is too often the case nowadays, I am interrupted by those who think they know best.

"That's long enough, dear," a cheerful voice announces. "The water's getting cold."

A heated towel draped over my shoulders, strong arms lift me out of my bath and in no time at all, I am dressed and back in my favourite reclining armchair, my feet toasty-warm in woolly boots, a blanket over my knees, waiting for my tea and biscuits.

*Now, where was I?*

After the air hostess has checked to make sure my seatbelt is securely fastened, I close my eyes and smile, a small gesture of secretive pleasure. Nobody here will ever know.

*They think I'm sleeping.*

Meanwhile, my flight is rocketing down the runway, gathering speed for take-off. Foreign destinations are calling.

# LOOK AT ME

My eyes are closed, but I hear them sneaking around on their rubber-soled shoes. When they pause at my bedside to update my clinical notes, I can feel their breath on me, but I don't react. Their analysis has been thorough, and they think they know all my secrets, but they don't. They don't even know I'm awake.

Of course, I shouldn't be here. That much is obvious to anyone with half a brain. Unfortunately for me, the magistrate, who committed me, was intimidated by my intellectual superiority. On the bright side, though, this facility no longer uses physical restraints of any kind. My so-called acute episodes are being managed with tranquilisers and antipsychotics, none of which I have ingested today – one more thing they don't know.

At 3am, while the night nurses are keeping each other company at the other end of the ward, I make my move. Once in the stairwell, I head for the roof. I'm going to show them – my parents, the magistrate, the doctors, the nurses and everyone else who has ever doubted me.

With a chilly breeze nibbling at edges of my light hospital gown, I position myself, arms outstretched on the edge of the rooftop, and take a moment to imagine their faces when they finally understand. It's not lunacy that empowers me, but genius.

I have another secret to reveal.

I can fly!

# JOURNEY'S END

Rolling the orange between my palms to loosen its skin, I wait. After magically converting months of sunshine into sweet-tasting flesh, this perfect orange is ripe for the eating. This one's for my mother; she loves them. Having grown up in a time of unremitting adversity, she has always been quick to remind me how fortunate I've been to live in a peaceful country where food is plentiful.

"When I was a girl," she would say. "I was lucky to get an orange at Christmas."

Perhaps that's why my father planted an orange tree for her when we first moved into our family home. This fat handful of an orange, then, this golden orb that warms my heart with childhood memories of backyard summers, is one of ours. My mother would appreciate that.

As I press my thumb into the top of the orange where the skin is thickest, its rind releases a fine zesty spray of oil that sweeps the smell of sadness aside and though my mother's eyes are cloudy with great age, they spark with recognition. She can smell it, too.

"What's that?" she manages to ask, her voice a weary traveller nearing journey's end.

I've been taking my time to peel the orange and break it into segments and now that I have her attention, I have something important to say before she leaves me.

"I love you, Mum," I tell her, and she rewards me with a juicy smile.

She knows.

# GOING HOME

Torn between a paralysing fear of obliteration and the primal urge to get home, she ventures out onto the first plank. She doesn't know how she got here or how this path can float like the bars of a psychedelic xylophone above the abyss, but at its end, she can just make out her goal. Even at a distance and despite the darkness, she recognises the portrait on the wall and her favourite porcelain teapot. If she can reach them, she will be home.

Ever so carefully, centimetre by centimetre, she crawls, commando style with her belly never leaving the implied security of the wooden surface of the path. She is a heartbeat away from the void and dares not look down. Her soul longs for it; her mind focuses on it and the iron in her blood draws her towards the magnetic pole of home. However, her progress is agonisingly slow and when she senses the trajectory of path shifting, she wails her despair into emptiness.

"Please. Let me go home," she moans.

Blinded by a sudden burst of intense light, she loses her grip and is swallowed by eternity.

Though her last words bring the medical team rushing to her bedside, they cannot save her. When a doctor examines her eyes, her pupils dilate and remain nonresponsive. The exact time of her death is duly noted.

# PATRIARCH

After a drawn-out family dispute, he has a conciliatory gift from his brother: tickets to the opening night of an Agatha Christie play, plush box seats and the promise of harmony in times to come. He couldn't be more pleased. He and his brother share a love of the theatre and especially whodunits. Rivals since boyhood, they always compete to see who spots the murderer first. However, he is confident. Noticing details, studying characters, analysing motives and putting all the pieces of a puzzle together are his forte and as his wife often reminds him, as patriarch of their family, he has had plenty of practice.

With the bar bells chiming, the theatre fills quickly, and his brother has not yet arrived to join him. He grows impatient.

The house lights have dimmed, and the curtain is rising when the door finally opens behind him. Turning to greet his brother, he is confronted instead by his nephew, who is holding a gun fitted with a silencer. Too late, the pieces fall into place. This, then, is how the rivalry between the brothers is to be finally resolved and peace within the family restored.

Tonight, he will be the victim and his nephew will be the murderer. After years of waiting, a new patriarch is emerging from the wings.

# FRESH IS BEST

Since moving from the city, Tara has enjoyed exploring the countryside. At the end of a long walk, she is delighted to discover a quaint stone cottage on the edge of the forest. It has the prettiest garden she has ever seen. Above the ground-hugging daisies and bluebells, showy foxgloves and delphiniums tremble in the breeze. Behind them an aromatic lavender hedge shelters under crepe myrtle trees that are dressed to impress in gorgeous ruffled trusses of pink, mauve and purple. The effect is so magical that Tara only notices the old woman in the shadows when she speaks.

"Hello, dear." the old woman says. "I haven't seen anyone out this way for a long time. Can I offer you a nice a cup of tea?"

As the old woman makes the tea, Tara admires the garden from the kitchen window. She wants to know how the old woman does it.

"Blood and bone, dear," the old woman replies without hesitation. "I swear by it."

Tara fancies starting a small garden of her own and asks, "Where do you buy it?"

"Oh no, dear, I don't buy it," the old woman replies, approaching Tara from behind. "Fresh is best."

With one deft stroke, she slits Tara's throat from ear to ear.

"I like to make my own".

# LEAVING

Laurel's mother can make anything. Though it has taken her many months, working by candlelight late into the night, she has transformed a few yards of bleached linen into an extraordinary wedding gown for her daughter. High-waisted with skirts floating on flounces and sprinkled with exquisitely embroidered forget-me-knots, Laurel's wedding dress is fit for a princess. As she smooths the fabric where it falls around Laurel's feet, her mother weeps. What will she do without her daughter?

Laurel's mother can make anything. Though tears may blur her vision, her hands work automatically, dipping into a basket of fragrant rosemary, plaiting it, entwining it with perfect pink rosebuds into a bridal wreath fit for a queen. Wrapped in golden memories of the past, Laurel's mother finds comfort in keeping busy. How can she let her daughter go?

Laurel's mother can make anything, but for all her love and care, she cannot make Laurel better. Leaning into Laurel's coffin, she kisses her daughter's icy cheek one last time. Enshrouded in bridal white and crowned with rosemary, Laurel is fit for Heaven.

# THE KNOWLEDGE

The day of his funeral dawns ominously dark. Instinctively – or perhaps from habit – when I take my black suit from its hanger, I lay it carefully on my side of our bed. As if it matters now. After four decades of marriage, his side is empty. He is gone.

Everything changed for us last year. Even after intensive therapy, the muscles on his right side were useless and on the other side, not much better. A stroke can do that. I was advised not to try to look after him at home, but who knew better how to look after him than me? I knew which foods he most enjoyed, the music that lifted his spirits, the television programs he never missed, exactly how he liked his cup of tea – and a million other little things about him. I knew everything that made his life worth living and after suffering years of marital abuse, I was given the chance to deprive him of the lot.

As it turns out, I thoroughly enjoyed our last year together, lording over him, denying him absolutely everything that brought him comfort or joy.

When the black limousine arrives, I wipe the ear-to-ear grin off my face, reinvent myself as the grieving widow and step outside as bright morning sunshine breaks through the clouds.

# DREAMER

When she goes to bed, she pats the empty space beside her and tunes in to talk back radio for company. She's never been one for music, but for her, the drone of lonely late night callers, reaching out to others across the airwaves or grinding their axes on the issues of the day, is as good as a lullaby and can send her off to sleep in minutes, but tonight is different.

As she is drifting to sleep, she is roused by a sharp burst of static from the radio and from somewhere deep within it, she imagines she hears him calling her name. A no-nonsense person, she chides herself for wishful thinking and hunkers further down under the covers, hoping to slip away again, but it happens once more and this time there's no mistaking it.

He is calling her. Every cell in her body aches for him, but she cannot believe, not even for a moment, that she is hearing his voice. After all, he has been gone for almost a year. Even so, she cannot resist the pull of her yearning, and as she reaches out to him in the darkness, deep in her chest where grief lies a leaden lump, a familiar warmth wraps itself around her heart and for the first time since his death, she is happy.

In the pink and grey hush of dawn, the dreamer slumbers on forever. She is at peace.

# PREVIOUSLY PUBLISHED

Thanks are given to publications in which these stories previously appeared in print or online:

*Dream Girl*, published online by Two Letter Press (defunct) *

*First Love*, published in *True Truth Serum Vol. 1*, Truth Serum Press, (Aust), 2017 (ed. Matt Potter)

*Fresh is Best*, published in *Three Drops from a Cauldron, Samhain 2015*, Three Drops Press (UK) 2015 (ed. Kate Garrett)+

*Midnight Feast*, published online by *Visible Ink* (Aust), July 2016

*Nightfall*, published online by *Field of Words*, also published in *Award Winning Australian Writing 2017 10th Anniversary Edition*, Melbourne Books (Aust.) 2017 (ed. Pia Gaardboe)<

*On Top of the World*, published in *Wiser Truth Serum Vol. 2*, Truth Serum Press (Aust) 2017 (ed. Matt Potter)

*Postulants*, published online by Jupiter Artland (UK) September 2015

*Sleeping Dogs*, published in *Hysteria 5*, Hysterectomy Association (UK) 2016 (ed. Lina Parkinson-Hardman)>

*Solstice*, published in *Three Drops from a Cauldron, Midwinter 2015*, Three Drops Press (UK) 2016 (ed. Kate Garrett)

*Stitch,* published in *Caterpillar Magazine* (Ireland), Summer 2016

*Tough Love,* published in *The School Magazine* Vol. 102 No. 8, NSW Department of Education (Aust), September 2017

*Mission Accomplished, Show Stopper* and *Tough Love* performed at *Tales after Dark,* Canberra, June 2016

*I Spy* performed at *Tales after Dark,* Canberra, September 2017

* winner Two Letter Press Flash Fiction Competition

+ runner-up in Australian Horror Writers' Association (AHWA) Flash fiction competition, 2015

< winner Field of Words Flash Fiction Competition, Round 2, 2016

> runner-up in Hysteria 2016 Writing Competition

# ACKNOWLEDGEMENTS

With many thanks to children's author, Sheryl Gwyther, who introduced me to the discipline of writing flash fiction, a genre where every word must work hard to justify its inclusion in a story. Also, thanks to the membership of the 52 Week Flash Fiction Challenge (about to enter its fourth year), especially Pat Simmons, Virginia Miranda, Rod Chadbourne, Faye Reavley and Lucy Drake for always inspiring me with generous feedback and encouragement. Last, to my local writers' group, The Stanhope Scribes, thanks for the company, conversation and coffee we enjoy as we hone our writing skills together.

# ABOUT THE AUTHOR

Irene Buckler taught in Australian primary schools for three decades. While teaching, she also wrote many educational programs, stories, plays and poetry for children. Her work has appeared in publications for children and teachers in the United Kingdom and in Australia, as well as online.

A flash fiction finalist in the 'Hysteria' (UK) and 'Field of Words' Writing Competitions (South Australia.), Irene is drawn by the challenge of writing flash fiction to be the very best writer she can be. Her flash fiction stories have been widely published in anthologies.

Residing in sunny Sydney with a couple of adult children, one dog, three cats, three budgerigars, one ring-tailed parrot and two rescued foxes, Irene plans her stories while taking long walks. A history buff, she also relishes those places, often the great cities of the world, such as Rome and London, where it is easy to reflect on today through the lens of the past.

A keen observer, Irene writes mainly about people, finding exploring human behaviour to be an endless source of inspiration.

# Also from TRUTH SERUM PRESS and PURE SLUSH BOOKS

http://truthserumpress.net/catalogue/

- *Kiss Kiss* by Paul Beckman
  978-1-925536-21-8 (paperback) 978-1-925536-22-5 (eBook)
- *Track Tales* by Mercedes Webb-Pullman
  978-1-925536-35-5 (paperback) 978-1-925536-36-2 (eBook)
- *On the Bitch* by Matt Potter
  978-1-925536-45-4 (paperback) 978-1-925536-46-1 (eBook)

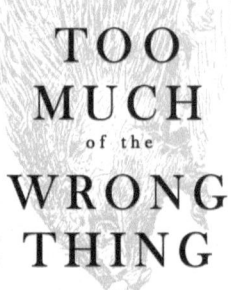

- *Happy² Pure Slush Vol. 15*
  978-1-925536-39-3 (paperback) 978-1-925536-40-9 (eBook)
- *Lust: 7 Deadly Sins Vol. 1*
  978-1-925536-47-8 (paperback) 978-1-925536-48-5 (eBook)
- *Too Much of the Wrong Thing* by Claire Hopple
  978-1-925536-33-1 (paperback) 978-1-925536-34-8 (eBook)

# Also from TRUTH SERUM PRESS and EVERYTIME PRESS

http://truthserumpress.net/catalogue/

- *All Roads Lead from Massilia* by Philip Kobylarz
  978-1-925536-27-0 (paperback)  978-1-925536-28-7 (eBook)
- *Wiser Truth Serum Vol. #2*
  978-1-925536-31-7 (paperback)  978-1-925536-32-4 (eBook)
- *True Truth Serum Vol. #1*
  978-1-925536-29-4 (paperback)  978-1-925536-30-0 (eBook)

- *Hello Berlin!* by Jason S. Andrews
  978-1-925536-11-9 (paperback)  978-1-925536-12-6 (eBook)
- *Deer Michigan* by Jack C. Buck
  978-1-925536-25-6 (paperback)  978-1-925536-26-3 (eBook)
- *Rain Check* by Levi Andrew Noe
  978-1-925536-09-6 (paperback)  978-1-925536-10-2 (eBook)

# Also from TRUTH SERUM PRESS

http://truthserumpress.net/catalogue/

- *Luck and Other Truths* by Richard Mark Glover
  978-1-925101-77-5 (paperback) 978-1-925536-04-1 (eBook)
- *happyme@t.us* by Kim Conklin
  978-1-925536-07-2 (paperback) 978-1-925536-08-9 (eBook)
- *What Came Before* by Gay Degani
  978-1-925536-05-8 (paperback) 978-1-925536-06-5 (eBook)

- *Based on True Stories* by Matt Potter
  978-1-925101-75-1 (paperback) 978-1-925101-76-8 (eBook)
- *The Miracle of Small Things* by Guilie Castillo Oriard
  978-1-925101-73-7 (paperback) 978-1-925101-74-4 (eBook)
- *La Ronde* by Townsend Walker
  978-1-925101-64-5 (paperback) 978-1-925101-65-2 (eBook)

www.ingramcontent.com/pod-product-compliance
Lightning Source LLC
Chambersburg PA
CBHW051839170626
46807CB00003B/1261